THE
EXECUTIVE

K.I. Lynn

USA TODAY BESTSELLING AUTHOR
K.I. LYNN

The Executive
Copyright © K.I. Lynn

Cover design by Lori Jackson Designs

Editor
Evident Ink
Marti Lynch
Danielle Leigh

Publication Date: January 30, 2019
Genre: FICTION/Romance/Contemporary
ISBN-13: 978-1-948284-06-6
Copyright © 2019 K.I. Lynn
All rights reserved

INSPIRATION PLAYLIST

There's No Way—Lauv feat. Julia Micheals

King of my Heart—Taylor Swift

8 Letters—Why Don't We

Lost in Japan—Shawn Mendes and Zedd

Head Above Water—Avril Lavigne

Youngblood—5 Second of Summer

Give You What You Want—Avril Lavigne

Slow Hands—Niall Horan

Like I'm Gonna Lose You—Meghan Trainor feat. John Legend

Lies in the Dark—Tove Lo

Way Down We Go—Kaleo

Tear You Apart—She Wants Revenge

Must Be the One—She Wants Revenge

Love Me Like You Do—Ellie Goulding

Take Me To Church—Hozier

OctaHate—Ryn Weaver

Bloodstream—Stateless

There You Are—Zayn

CHAPTER 1

Ivy

I T WAS GOING TO BE A GOOD DAY. AT LEAST, AS SOON AS I was out the door. I could feel it deep in my bones—today was my day.

It was my day to be offered a new position and finally quit working for the womanizing asshole. Maybe the grass wasn't greener on the other side, but I no longer wanted to work for someone without morals any longer. The environment was toxic, and I was tired of fighting off unwanted advances.

The clock was almost hypnotizing, the second hand captivating. I watched it tick around, passing numbers, running down the minutes until I left, making me zone out and jump when the phone rang. Everything around me came back into focus, and I quickly picked up the receiver.

"Good afternoon, Ivy Prescot, assistant to Dante Kilgore." Ugh, I hated the way I had to answer the phone. It was such a mouthful, but those were my instructions.

"Hello, Ivy. Mike Deacon, here." It was a familiar and

welcome voice.

A genuine smile crept onto my face. "Mike! How are you doing?"

"Fine, fine. How's Dante treating you today?"

The conversation brought me out of my zoning, and I started going through the new emails. "Same as always. Like I owe him time between my legs."

"Unfortunate."

I made a noise of agreement. "What can I do for you, Mike?" I asked. It was unusual for Mike to call instead of his assistant.

"I need to cancel our lunch next week. We'll set up something in a few weeks."

I pulled up Dante's calendar and flipped to next week, finding the Wednesday appointment. "That's too bad. Why didn't Stephanie call me?"

"Unlike other CEOs, I'm fully capable of pulling up a number. Plus, there is the added bonus of hearing your sweet voice."

"Flattery. You're just trying to make me feel good before Dante goes off."

A soft chuckle. "He is rather impetuous."

Something about the cancellation bothered me, and I couldn't help scratching the itch. "May I ask why? This has been in the works for months."

"You really are quite perceptive. Honestly, I don't like the way he handles things. I would have left negotiations long ago if it hadn't been for you, but I've been hearing rumors."

I tried to ignore the part about me. It wasn't a romantic sentiment, definitely professional, but still it made me wonder. "Rumors? Really?"

Another chuckle. "You can't hide the glee in your voice,

young lady."

"Calling me young lady. Fourteen years older than me isn't that bad, you know." I slapped my hand over my mouth while I questioned my sanity. Flirting? Really, Ivy? You have Peter, remember?

"Don't tempt me," Mike said, his voice lower than before. Almost suggestive.

I was almost speechless. "Have a good day, Mike."

"You, too."

As I hung up the phone, I let out a sigh. Mike was a gentleman. He even had the distinguished look with a little bit of salt in his hair. Handsome, polite, and somehow, I couldn't help flirting with him, just a little.

Perhaps it was because he saw me as a person, not just a pussy. Or maybe it was just that Mike Deacon made me swoon. I didn't normally swoon over men.

"Ivy, where are the financial reports for last quarter?" Dante yelled from his office.

I was tempted to ignore him, to continue working until he noticed the file sitting in front of him. Then again, I was fairly certain he'd been distracted by an intern hiding under his desk when I set it down.

"Ivy!"

With a sigh I grabbed my laptop and a notebook.

"Have you checked your desk?" I asked as I walked in.

His eyes narrowed, then down to his desk and the file.

No *sorry* or *thanks*. Never. Always expectation.

"The numbers aren't great," I said as I sat in a chair across from his desk.

"Fuck," he cursed under his breath. "Why do I pay a sales team if they can't fucking bring in new accounts?"

I was so incredibly tempted to respond, but instead, I bit my tongue. The sales team wasn't the problem. They did bring in potential clients. It was Dante who couldn't close the deal.

Dante was actually a good-looking man, yet his personality was disgusting. The quintessential handsome man with dark brown hair, vibrant blue eyes, and a chiseled jaw. He liked to have a "personal relationship" with all of his clients. At least that was the bullshit he spewed dazzling them with his charming smile.

Many had been snared in the web of charm. Many signed contracts.

Unfortunately, his dick always got in the way of business, causing him to cancel lunch meetings to fuck whatever random girls he had on the side.

All those cancelled meetings resulted in pissed-off people who didn't sign new contracts. Lately Dante's ego had taken over, and he let customer interaction slide. He was the boss, after all, and therefore, he could do whatever he wanted.

The numbers told a different story, and this rat was ready to abandon ship for more than one reason.

"At least we have Chandelier set up to sign next week," he said as he closed the file.

"About that…" I trailed off.

He groaned and leaned back in his chair. "What now?"

"Mike Deacon just called and cancelled lunch for next week."

"Cancelled? Did he say why?"

I shook my head. "He's consulting his calendar for a new date."

"Shit. We're never going to close this deal." He let out a sigh.

I said nothing. There was no reason to bring up what I knew. Rather, I liked seeing him stew. Mike wasted months talking to Dante. Then he realized Dante would never be able to deliver the sort of attention to detail a company like Chandelier demanded.

I scanned over the calendar as I tapped my pen against the armrest. "Newlyn is coming on Monday."

Dante sat straight up, a determined look settling on his angular face. "Newlyn. That's the department store chain, right?"

I nodded. "They have over two hundred locations and are rapidly expanding."

"If we can get ahold of them, that could be long term." He strummed his fingers against the wood top of his desk for a minute before looking to me. "Why don't you come over to my house this weekend so we can work on the pitch?"

And it begins. "We can work on that Friday during business hours."

He ignored me and attempted to sweeten the idea. "I can order from that Italian place you love."

"*You* love Eduardo's, not me," I reminded him.

He waved his hand in the air. "Whatever. We can order a nice dinner."

"Dinner?" I asked with a quirked brow. I would never work with him on the weekend, let alone at his home, so it was somewhat entertaining to watch him flounder. Almost as if he would find something that would make me fall for it.

"Or lunch, and we can work our way to dinner." He grinned at me.

"I don't think so."

"Come on, Ivy," he said with a smirk. "You can't resist me forever."

"Watch me." I glanced up at the clock behind him and cursed. "Shit!"

He glanced behind him, then back to me. "Something wrong?"

I jumped up and gathered my notebook, stacking my laptop and the files together. "I have a doctor's appointment in thirty minutes," I said. Though the doctor part was a lie, I did have an appointment I couldn't miss.

His brow scrunched. "Did you tell me?"

I rolled my eyes. The man never listened to me. Captain of what was plainly obvious if he ever bothered to pay attention. "Last Thursday, Monday, yesterday, and this morning. I even put it in your calendar." He would be doomed without me, and after five years of bullshit, I couldn't help but smile at the thought.

"Why can't you make these appointments for after work?" he asked, clearly annoyed.

"Because they're only open until five." I rolled my eyes. Sometimes I wondered how the man tied his own shoes. Then again, I'd been doing everything for him for years, and there were probably other women taking care of him before that.

Dante was nothing but a man-child with a teenage libido and an entitled mindset.

"Fine. We'll talk about this weekend in the morning."

"No, we won't."

"Always so feisty."

"Don't chase me."

"That makes me want to chase you more."

"I'll just run faster." I waved my hand in the air as I made my way out the door. "See you tomorrow."

The second the stack from my hands was on my desk, I

grabbed my jacket and purse, and was out the door.

Once in my car, I pulled out my phone and noticed a missed text message.

Good luck today. You got this!—Peter

I smiled down at my phone before slipping it back into my purse. I'd only been dating Peter a couple of weeks, but he was a nice guy and we had fun together.

Traffic was always a pain and I was a few minutes behind when I pulled into a parking garage across the street and found a spot. The few sparse minutes I had remaining to get inside and up had my pulse pumping as I speed walked across the street.

My heart pounded in my chest as I walked up to the towering seventy-six stories of the Columbia Center. The sun reflected off the huge windows that encased the interior, almost blinding me.

For five years I had worked my ass off, waiting for a promotion and a decent raise that was always out of reach. All because I wouldn't sleep with my boss. Passed over to reward those who kept his dick wet or were one of the boys.

A change was long overdue, but I was comfortable. One late night and a handsy executive who thought my thighs should spread for him, and I'd officially had enough. Pushing Dante away was almost a game after all these years, but I no longer felt safe after hours.

Data Consolidation Services, or DCS, was a data collection and cloud service company with in-house software design tailored to its clientele, and similar to Kilgore Industries. The difference was DCS was a serious company while Kilgore was more Dante's playground.

The head of DCS was Lincoln Devereux, a young and

driven CEO who quadrupled the company's revenue in the six years since he took over.

He was an icon of brains and an idol of looks. He embodied the sexy executive look, with perfectly styled hair, strong jaw, and piercing eyes. It didn't hurt that his perfectly tailored suits accentuated his strength.

I may or may not have stalked his photos when researching the company before my first interview. And then maybe a little after. He didn't have a Facebook account or Instagram that I could find, but there were still photos of him everywhere. There was article after article about his accomplishments with DCS, but sparse when it came to his personal life.

He was also very giving in his yearly donations, and not just the company, but with his own money as well. I still swooned over the fact that he gave so much money to The London Foundation, a charity to help survivors of suicide or the families they left behind. One hundred students' tuitions were covered for one year at the University of Washington.

I still couldn't believe that the position for his executive assistant had been open for months and that, with the possibly hundreds of candidates, I'd made it through all the hoops to an interview with the man himself.

My palms were already sweating, heart hammering in my chest as I made my way through the three-story glass and marble entry. It was light and airy and filled with the bustle of a busy afternoon. There were shops in the atrium as well as on the second floor.

A chirp filled my ears, and I turned to see two birds chasing each other around the potted trees growing in what appeared to be an indoor grove.

I was captivated watching the birds in my power-walked

to the elevator, and I wasn't looking in front of me. I barely caught the grey color in my periphery before slamming into an arm and chest. The hit left me off balance and gravity took over.

My future flashed before my eyes and I saw myself sprawled out across the floor, before something grabbed me and I spun, ending in a dip like a perfectly choreographed dance. Though I was certain I didn't look nearly as elegant.

I blinked, wide-eyed, at the man who caught me as my heart slammed and adrenaline pumped through my veins.

"Hello, beautiful," he said as he brushed a strand of hair from my face.

"I-I'm so sorry."

I stared up at the man who caught me, and was struck stupid.

I slammed into Lincoln Devereux.

My brain short circuited, because Lincoln-*fucking*-Devereux had his arms around me, and there were some serious sparks flying. Photos did not do him justice. The man was so much more handsome in person.

"No need. Are you all right?"

"Yes, thank you."

He was beautiful. Elegant and regal in a crisp charcoal suit. Slowly he straightened and planted me firmly back on my feet. Then I noticed the men he was with, all in equally expensive crisp suits. I felt the heat flush across my face.

"Thank you so much. Again, I'm so sorry," I apologized profusely. Why did it have to be him? My stomach was so tight I felt nauseous.

"It's fine," he said as he looked me over. "No blood."

"It's all in my face."

He chuckled. "That it is."

He fished into his pocket and pulled out a business card holder. After borrowing a pen, he began writing on the back. "If you need someone to watch over you tonight to make sure you're okay, give me a call." He winked at me. "I'd be more than happy to make sure the blood has receded. I'll be very thorough in my inspection." He held the card out. "My personal number is on the back."

I stared down at the card in shock, trying not to notice the way my body tingled at just the thought.

"Okay. Have a good day."

Have a good day? Way to sound like a complete idiot, Ivy.

He smiled at me, that blinding, seductive type that makes women go weak a the knees, and returned to his companions.

I watched after him, trying to settle down and not fawn over the fact that he gave me his number. Granted, it was an invitation for sex, but still, I was floored.

Lincoln Devereux really was a god.

I was in a bit of a daze as I made my way to the elevator and up to Amy in HR. We went over a few things and she gave me a few pointers, all of which went in one ear and out the other because of the way my skin still tingled from his touch.

It wasn't until she led me down to his office a few minutes later that reality kicked back in. Suddenly, I was a mess. There was already panic settling in knowing I was meeting with him, but after the encounter in the lobby what would his reaction be to seeing me again? Would I be the idiot girl who made a fool out of herself, or would he find it entertaining?

The girl manning the desk outside his office had a frightened look on her face, her hair a mess as she searched the desk for her phone.

"Mr. Devereux, your four o'clock is here," she said with a squeak.

Her demeanor was one of utter chaos, and by the state of the desk, the position was in desperate need of me.

The girl opened the door for me before quickly scurrying away like a frightened mouse.

I took a steadying breath before stepping through the door.

CHAPTER 2

Lincoln

A SOFT FLORAL SCENT FILLED MY SENSES BEFORE A LIGHT lilt invaded my ears.

"Good afternoon, Mr. Devereux."

Something about the way she said my name enticed me. All of it was familiar, but new. I turned toward the stranger in my office and understood. The beauty I'd had in my arms not twenty minutes prior stood in front of me looking like sin delivered on a silver platter for me to devour.

Fuck. My jaw ticked in agitation. I was looking forward to spending the evening between her thighs, not offering her a job. It'd been weeks since I'd gotten off, and I was as turned on by her now as I was in the lobby.

"Miss Preston, I take it?"

"Prescot, actually, sir," she corrected me.

I sat back at my desk without even a handshake. She had the most delicious curves. Touching her would result in so much more than the simple greeting warranted. "I can say it's a surprise to see you before me right now. It's a far cry from what I envisioned when I slipped you my card."

Her cheeks began to pink, eyes staring. There it was, the attraction I'd sensed.

"I hope what happened in the lobby doesn't have any ill effect on my interview."

"Of course not," I said as I gestured for her to sit.

I had no idea who she was past her name and resume, but after our encounter in the lobby, my dick was very interested in getting to know her.

Ivy Prescot was my newest interviewee and the most potential trouble to me.

I stared as she sat. Her blue eyes were wide, surrounded by a modest amount of makeup. Her face was framed by silky brown waves that extended past her shoulders. My fingers itched to feel the strands between them. The vision of me pounding into her from behind while I knotted my hand into her hair and pulled was intoxicating.

Fuck her, and not in the sexual sense.

I was hard watching her squirm under my scrutiny. The way her eyes turned from my gaze, her cheeks pinked as she nibbled her plump bottom lip told me I had as much of an effect on her.

I began to wonder if I could tell her she wouldn't be a good fit in this position, but I could make it fit in another. Would she slap me? Would she be able to grasp my double entendre? Or would that pink deepen and spread. Those beautiful blues darken, silently begging me?

"You've made it pretty far, and by HR's standards, you would have been hired. However, there's been a rotating door in the position as of late, and I'm tired of trying to break in new assistants who can't handle the pressure and are gone in a few weeks."

"Understandable. A man in your position holds a lot of weight on your shoulders. A good assistant is needed to help you balance that weight."

It was just the cut-to-the-chase start of the interview, but her response to a non-question was impressive.

"I'm not easy to work for. My demands are high, as are my expectations. This company didn't grow so much these last few years because I was sitting on my ass. Therefore, I don't need someone to just get me coffee and take my calls. I need a right-hand man, or woman in this case."

Silence stretched between us. It was obvious in her expression, the way she stared at me, how she was almost bursting to say something, and it was probably not on topic. Apparently the shock had worn off.

I sighed and sat back, wanting to get whatever was on her mind out so that we could move on. "Speak."

She blinked at me. "Excuse me?"

"It's obvious you are dying to say something. Say it."

Her face lit up. "Mr. Devereux, what you did, by giving all that money to—"

I held up my hand and cut her off. "Never mind. Shut up," I said as the vein on my temple began to throb. "I don't need you waxing poetic on my accomplishments. I did them, ergo I know."

"Yes, sir, you are absolutely correct."

I quirked a brow at her. It wasn't the response I was expecting nor what I was used to. "This is your resume?" I asked, shaking the page in front of her.

Her brow furrowed. "Y-yes?"

"It either is or it isn't," I said through clenched teeth. Her indecision could be an annoying trait, much like her fuckability.

"Seeing as it is a random sheet of paper you picked up from your desk, I can only assume it is my resume," she replied with more snark than I expected. "Sir."

"Hmph." That caught me off guard. I'd forgotten fuckwit number eight placed it on my desk before Miss Prescot arrived.

Truth was, I hadn't read it since I selected her from the stack of resumes. HR set everything up, including conducting initial interviews and tests. For years I had a great assistant, Amanda, but I lost her to a baby a year ago. Since then HR had sent over a string of idiots, and I demanded final say.

Miss Prescot intrigued me already, and for more than a one-night stand.

Scanning the page, which included notes from HR, I was reminded why she'd made it in front of me—college graduate in business, scored the highest I'd seen in the company aptitude tests, and she had five years working for that shithead, Dante Kilgore. He was known to be slimy, fucking any employee who would let him.

He was also my best friend long ago, before we became rivals. I took no prisoners, and friends, ex or not, were no exception. Especially Dante.

Setting the page down, I looked back to Miss Prescot. "Why the desire to leave Kilgore Industries for one of their competitors?"

"I feel as if I've learned all that I can from Dante, and I want more," she said without missing a beat.

"More what? Do you want to be more than an assistant?"

"I want to be more of an aide-de-camp and not a transcribing coffee getter. I want to work with someone who sees my value and respects my insights."

"That takes time." I was more impressed by her use of aide-de-camp than anything else.

"If in five years the transition still hasn't happened, it's not going to. Therefore, I need to leave. I want to help DCS become the absolute leader of this industry."

"It will take time. At least six months, and you will be getting me coffee."

"I understand. I'll be starting over. There's always a learning curve, even in the same industry."

I carefully studied her reactions and response to my questions. The thought that she could be here as a spy had crossed my mind, but I sensed an edge of disdain in many of her responses.

"I'm going to be blunt—have you ever fucked Dante?"

Her eyes popped wide, her mouth falling open. "Does everyone know about him?"

It wasn't the response I was hoping for and anger began to seep in. I certainly didn't want Dante's sloppy seconds in any sense. "Answer the question, or leave."

"No. Hell, no," she vehemently denied, her voice firm.

Relief washed through me, but still I wondered. "What makes you the rare bird to escape his clutches?"

"A backbone? A desire to live disease free?"

"Is that why you want to leave his employ?"

"He's not the only unsavory character there, and I don't want to deal with them anymore. I shouldn't have to. And may I be perfectly frank?" she asked. I nodded, and she continued. "I have far too much self-worth to demean myself with a man who propositions his employees without thought or concern for his company's well-being. It's not the right place for me or my talents."

Her words didn't surprise me, I knew about Dante's personality. Yet, her candid recall and admission was impressive.

"No, you shouldn't, at all. You don't have to worry about that here," I assured her, though I wasn't certain I could live up to that promise. However, I also wasn't like Dante. If something did happen, it would be because she wanted it.

"And why is that? Am I the wrong gender?"

A chuckle sprang from me, and I couldn't help the smile that began to spread. "Very much not gay, but I also like to think I have a bit more decorum than that Neanderthal."

"An ant has more decorum than Dante."

I couldn't help but chuckle again. "You're very beautiful, and I'm no saint, but I have a feeling once you start working for me, you won't want anything to do with me."

"Once I start?"

The words had fallen from my mouth before I could even process what they meant. She'd caught me off guard. I liked her responses, and she had shown me that she did have the backbone she claimed.

"The position is yours."

"What? Just like that?" she asked in bewilderment.

I pushed back and stood in front of her. "You made me laugh and appear to be competent. I'm not looking for help in the bedroom; there are other women for that." I held out my hand. "There is a thirty-day trial period. If you make it past that point there is a raise. Another thirty days, another raise. I'm not easy to work for and many haven't made it past sixty days. Those who have were exceptional. If you shake my hand, you accept and I will have the contract drawn up."

She stared up at me, then down to my hand. "I like a

challenge," she said as she slipped her hand in mine.

I tried not to think about how soft her hand felt. About how good it would feel wrapped around my shaft. About how good she would feel under me.

Every thought in my mind was overruled by the desire to take her.

"Mr. Devereux?" she asked after I hadn't released her hand.

I cleared my throat and let go. "You will start Monday."

She froze. "But that's only three days' notice."

"Do you need a recommendation from a man who only sees you as a hole to fuck?"

She was silent for a moment before she spoke. "No."

"Good. Be here Monday at seven-thirty."

"Monday at seven-thirty," she repeated.

"Someone will be in touch this evening with the contract. Let me know if there are any issues. I look forward to beginning our relationship."

"Thank you very much, sir. I look forward to working with you." Her smile was genuine, and I attempted to etch it into my memory.

The moment she began working for me, that smile would disappear.

As soon as she was out the door, I walked over to the wet bar and poured two fingers of whiskey. The burn as it slid down my throat did nothing to quell the fire licking at every inch of my body and mind.

I hadn't felt that charged in years.

Miss Prescot was everything I needed in a personal assistant, and everything I didn't. Mixing business and pleasure was something I avoided, but I knew I wasn't going to be able to with her around.

Perhaps I shouldn't have offered her the position, but in three months of interviews, her qualifications and personality had exceeded all the others. I was tired of the revolving door or temporary assistants that couldn't wipe their own ass, let alone get me a decent cup of coffee.

All of that, and I also wanted an inside look at Dante's business. I *needed* it.

I was prepared to destroy anyone and anything that got in my way.

Phone in hand, I pulled up my contacts and found the one I was looking for. It rang twice before a familiar voice picked up.

"Hello?"

"Marcus, I think we have our in," I said.

There was a slight pause as he registered what I meant, not even questioning why I called instead of emailed as I was supposed to. "How?"

"I just hired his assistant as my own."

"She doesn't have an NDA or non-compete clause?" he asked, and I heard rustling in the background.

Damn, I didn't ask.

"I'm not certain about the NDA, but Dante is so full of himself I'm sure he thinks no woman would ever quit working for someone as wonderful as him to work for one of his competitors."

"True. What if this is a ploy?"

"While not below his level, I don't think he'd give up the person who probably knows the inner workings better than him, even for an advantage."

"From what I've found, he might."

"Fine, then I'll figure out a way to make certain." I poured more liquid into the glass.

"You're going to fuck with her, aren't you?"

"If that's what it takes." Though I'd fuck her regardless. Everything else was collateral damage. "This is who I've been waiting for."

"His assistant?"

"Any in." I threw back the glass, letting the liquid slide down my throat. "I'll finally bring Dante down to his fucking knees."

I ended the call and began looking through my contacts, searching for the evening's date. Someone needed to alleviate my situation and it sure as hell wasn't going to be my hand.

CHAPTER 3

Ivy
Two weeks later

"I NEED THE BUG REPORT FROM THE NEWEST CS diagnostic update along with the reports for the Black Spell account," Mr. Devereux said as he typed an email, not even looking at me.

Mr. Devereux wasn't joking when he said he was difficult to work for. The charismatic man who held me in his arms and offered me a night with him was very different from Mr. Devereux, my boss.

Perhaps working for Dante wasn't so bad after all. Then again, I liked that Mr. Devereux treated me as more than a skirt with no brains. Well, some days he treated me like I had no brains.

I so wanted to be a fly on the wall that first week after I left. For a final, *fuck you, Dante*, I made no notes, nothing but the calendar held the day's agenda. He left me a scathing voicemail.

"You're screwing me over for an unscrupulous man who will destroy you."

It was an odd thing to say, and I could only interpret it as more of his rivalry with Mr. Devereux spilling out. In all the time I'd worked for him, Dante never like Mr. Devereux. I believed it was because he was angry, scared even, when clients left Kilgore in favor of DCS.

I reached into the stack in my hand and pulled out a file. "Here is the CS diagnostic. It came a few minutes ago. And I'll contact support for Black Spell."

He glanced down at the file, then back to his monitors. "Just don't talk to that idiot Davidson. I want last month and this month." He pointed to his coffee cup. "This is empty."

"I'll get a refill right away." I'd learned the hard way that I needed to walk around his desk to pick his cup up. What would forever be known as the disastrous coffee incident was so for two different reasons.

The first mistake I made was ordering it to be delivered. A week in and I was still getting the hang of things. I'd barely set the cup on his desk when he took a sip and immediately put it back down.

"What the fuck is that?" he spat, his mouth turned down in disgust.

"I'm sorry, is it wrong?"

"If there's enough sugar in my coffee to kill a diabetic elephant, then yes, it sure is fucking wrong." He stared down in disgust at the cup. *"What did you put in it?"*

"I ordered it from downstairs."

He stopped and narrowed his eyes. *"There's an espresso machine ten feet from you and exact instructions taped to it."*

"I don't know how to use it."

"*Then figure it out. Get this shit out of my sight and get me a coffee. Now.*"

"*Yes, sir.*" *I reached across the desk and grabbed the cup.*

I still didn't know if I squeezed it too hard, or if the lid had popped when he took the caustic sip, but the dark liquid sloshed out all over his desk and the sleeve of his jacket.

"*Fuck,*" *he cursed as he jumped up, swinging his jacket off.*

"*Oh, my God, I'm so sorry, sir.*"

"*Sorry isn't an excuse for stupidity.*"

"*It was an accident.*"

"*Perhaps, but you've ruined the papers on my desk.*" He tossed his jacket at me, and I barely managed to catch it without spilling more of the coffee. "*Get that cleaned and back by lunch.*"

"*But that's only thirty minutes,*" *I argued.*

"*And before you do that, clean up this fucking mess. Get going, Miss Prescot.*"

Two weeks in, and I was frantically juggling all the new information with keeping his days organized and obtaining the often obscure information he needed with little guidance or reference. The acronyms alone kept me busy. There had been a crash course, and a necessary cheat sheet created.

There was a binder left from his last assistant. However, over the past year since her departure, all the fill-ins, temps, and failures had scratched, ripped, and left it an almost unreadable, unreliable mess.

Thankfully, I made a friend. She worked a few floors down for one of the mid-level executives and I bumped into her one day my first week while lost. She was kind enough to help me that day and guide me since.

"If it's not in his personal file, it's on the shared drive," she said over the phone.

For twenty minutes I'd looked for the Black Spell account information after the manager of support told me it was in the account file, then hung up on me. I got the impression that the slew of predecessors before me left a bad taste in many mouths, and they all assumed that I was going to be gone just as they were.

"Open that, then the client folder, find the name, and inside you should find almost every document he will ever want."

I scribbled down some notes while I clicked through her directions. "Thank you so much, Alex."

"No problem. I've got an opening for lunch at noon. You?"

I scanned the calendar and found a possible opening. "If you can wait a few minutes I think I can run away about fifteen after."

She chuckled over the line. "I can wait."

Every day the minutes flew by. I liked being busy, but every second I was in the office, my body buzzed. Almost like I was in anticipation, waiting for something, but I didn't know what that was. Maybe it was the anxiety manifesting itself into a physical response. Whatever it was, there was never a spare second to even breathe. If the phone wasn't ringing, it was an email popping up, or a meeting I needed to accompany him to while I also fielded emails and kept detailed notes.

Never had I been so equipped either. I was used to a laptop and a phone with Dante. Working at DCS, I had a tablet, phone, computer, and all were synced together, allowing information to transfer instantly. It was a bit of a learning curve, but it did make things a lot easier.

The door to the office opened, but I was too engrossed in finishing my email to look up.

"Umm, Miss Prescot?" a small voice called out, drawing

my attention.

I glanced up to find a waifish-looking blonde girl. Her large brown eyes blinked behind black wire frames, and she had a skittish aura about her.

"Yes?"

"Hi, I'm Stacey Collins, the intern?" There was absolutely no confidence in her voice, and I suddenly pitied the girl.

I vaguely remembered an email about an incoming intern, but there was so much information to absorb that I'd completely forgotten about it.

"Hello. Please, call me Ivy." I held out my hand, and she lightly slipped hers in. "I'm so sorry, I completely forgot you were coming, so I'm not sure what to do at the moment."

"Oh, I just came to introduce myself. There is an intern introduction today."

I blew out a breath and smiled at her. "That's good. It will give me time to prepare. You will be here Monday, right?"

She nodded.

"I look forward to it," I said, making sure to give her my friendliest smile.

She gave a small wave as she headed out. I stared after her, afraid she might faint before she got out the door. How had she secured an internship with Lincoln Devereux? He was going to eat her alive.

Immediately I started an email to maintenance so that she could have a desk to work from, then an email to tech support for a computer and setup. Supposedly it was to be taken care of by the intern program, but I needed it done now and not sometime next week. Being the CEO's assistant had its perks sometimes, and that included getting whatever I needed ASAP.

"I'll be back in time for the two o'clock shareholder

meeting," Mr. Devereux said as he rushed past, not even glancing at me.

The door that led to Mr. Devereux's office was usually open, and he always managed to scare me when he suddenly appeared in front of my desk. Were the floors soundproof?

"Have a good lunch," I called after him.

He turned and smirked. "Oh, I will."

I hated the sinking feeling that occupied my stomach. The calendar simply said "Lunch—Yvette," and I knew it wasn't a business lunch. No, those were more complicated, like tomorrow's "Lunch—Armando's. Sean Thomas, Intercontinental Express."

After finishing up my email, I gave Alex a quick phone call and arranged to meet her in the lobby.

Alex was a petite woman in her mid-thirties with light brown hair down to her waist that she always kept back in a loose ponytail or loose half-braid. She was cheery, and the only bright spot of my day.

We didn't wander far for lunch, but that was because there were a dozen great options within a block or two.

"How is it you didn't get this position?" I asked as I scarfed down my chicken Caesar salad.

Another of her light giggles escaped as she shook her head. "No way would I work for that man. Stephen already keeps me busy, and he's many notches below Lincoln. My husband would like the money, but not the hours or the stress."

She wasn't kidding about either of those. My first week I worked forty-eight hours and crashed every night I got home. I was already at fifty for the week and still had half of Friday left.

"I really can't thank you enough for all your help these last couple of weeks."

She waved her hand. "I'm happy to help."

"Did you help the ones before me?"

She shook her head. "No. Some of them really were idiots. I questioned how HR even let them through, but maybe the application pool was low. I did try at first, but soon found I was doing a lot of their job *and* my job while getting none of the perks."

"Glad to know I'm not an idiot," I said with a laugh.

"Oh, you're not. I like helping you because usually I'm just directing you to what you need, not doing it for you. Totally different."

We were able to take our time at lunch, which was nice for a change, before returning to the office.

I was barely back at my desk when the phone rang and I stretched to pick it up.

"Lincoln Devereux's office." My greeting was so much easier than before.

"Well, my, my. I know that voice. Hello, Ivy," a familiar voice said across the line.

"Mike?" I asked in surprise.

"The rumors were true."

"Very. How are you?" I asked, unable to keep the smile from my face.

"Well. You? Are things different for you there?"

"Very. Demanding has taken on a whole new definition."

"Oh, I have no doubt."

"What can I do for you?" I knew why he was calling, but it was polite to ask anyway.

"I've officially cancelled all contract negotiations with Kilgore and I'd like to see what DCS has to offer."

"I'm sure Mr. Devereux will be happy to hear that. When

are you available?"

With some finagling, we were able to find an opening a few weeks out that worked for both of their schedules.

A few minutes after hanging up with Mike, Mr. Devereux returned.

"Welcome back," I said as he entered.

He said nothing, but quirked a brow at me. "Aren't you going to ask how my lunch was?"

"How was your lunch?" I asked with a fake smile plastered on my face. I really didn't want to know, but for some reason, he wanted me to.

"Succulent and juicy," he said with a lick of his lips.

Again, my stomach fell. "Great."

"Have you caught up on the data collection protocol?" he asked, back to business. Looking at him, he didn't seem any more relaxed than when he left, which was odd for a man who just got his rocks off. Maybe she wasn't any good.

"Almost. I have a few questions."

He continued into his office, and I followed behind him. "Good. We can go over them later. The faster you know this company, the better."

"Why do companies want to collect so much information?"

He stopped and turned back to me. "You worked for Dante for five years and you can't answer that question?"

"I understand for marketing and product targeting."

"Analysis, information, and storage capabilities is what we provide. Every time you scan that frequent-shopper card, it gets filtered through, compared, so the company can target you with customized ads and promotions that are more apt to get you into the store. Specialty service companies need software to process their inventory and organize their clients' tastes and preferences. We create the software to handle all of their needs as well as information storage."

"It's just that, reading the data collection information, I wonder why people give up so much privacy."

"Good question, but that is the evolution of the technological age. You use your smartphone to pay your bill—that was me."

"What do you mean that was you?"

"It was the program I created that got me this position. The program that skyrocketed DCS. Shopper cards have been around for twenty years, but they hadn't evolved. Now, there are grocery store apps with digital coupons. It not only cuts down on paper waste, but now businesses have all the customer and product information they need all in one system."

Wow. I knew that he was a revered software developer, but somehow I didn't know the list of industry accomplishments that were directly related to his efforts.

"Do you miss being a software developer?"

He glanced at me and gave a small smile. "Sometimes. Then I remind myself of my goal and how I can only accomplish that as CEO." He grabbed his tablet and his leather portfolio. "I want a coffee waiting when I get back."

"Yes, sir."

He strode past me to his shareholder meeting. All the while, my mind turned his words. While yes, I did know most of the answers to what seemed like inane questions, I was curious to hear *his* answers. We'd spent so little time getting to know one another, and I wasn't sure he realized that hindered my ability to properly do my job. Perhaps the dozen before me inspired so little confidence that he didn't want to open up to me, but I was determined to change that.

I wanted to know Lincoln Devereux. More than the handsome leader with an eye for development, but the man.

Moreover, I wanted to know his goals. By his admission, I had a strong suspicion it had nothing to do with DCS.

⤫

A few days later, I was stuck in traffic on my way into the office, when my sister, Iris, called. Thankfully, she phoned after I was up. She had a tendency to forget I was three hours behind her.

"How's the job going?" she asked.

"As well as can be expected," I replied with a yawn. The long hours were getting better but my body was still begging for sleep.

"Uh-oh, what does that mean?"

"It's just, well, the transition period is harder than I expected," I admitted before taking a sip of my coffee and wishing all the cars would disappear so I could get to work before I fell asleep. "There wasn't really anyone to help me get going. Kind of a sink-or-swim situation."

By the way my interview went, I expected we would get along and that he would help me understand him and DCS. However, it seemed like he avoided me more than anything. That avoidance created friction and things needed to change before something happened.

"I totally would have drowned."

Yes, she would have. "It's fine," I said with a sigh as I downed the last of my cup. "I'm just exhausted."

"You sound it."

"How's Jeremy?" I asked, steering the conversation away from me. There was no more coffee and I was in desperate need for more. I needed to get to the lobby Starbucks, stat.

"We broke up last week."

"What? Why didn't you call me?" Iris always called or texted me about everything.

"Because I wasn't beaten up about it or anything."

"A few weeks ago, you were falling in love with him," I reminded her.

"Yeah, well, that was more with his dick than anything else about him."

Bingo. Sometimes her libido was stronger than her head. "Ah, you were infatuated with the D, not the man."

"Speaking of D—how's what's his name?"

It took me way too long to even figure out who she was talking about, because the first person who came to mind was Mr. Devereux. While I hadn't had any experience with his D, that didn't mean I didn't think about it. A lot more than I should, given his shitty attitude toward me.

"Peter?" It hit me, and much later than it should have.

"Yeah, him."

Peter gave up on me before I'd even finished my first two weeks at DCS. We'd celebrated with dinner after I got the position, but that was the last time I saw him.

"I got a voicemail the other day. We're done."

There was a gasp on the other end. "He broke up with you over voicemail?"

I sighed as I pulled into the parking garage. "I don't blame him. We'd only gone on a handful of dates and then I get this job and I didn't have the time or energy to contact him."

"New boss is working you to the bone."

"Yep."

"You're not sad, though." It wasn't a question, but a

statement. She was completely right. I didn't have much to be sad over. Peter was a nice guy, but if he called it quits that easily, there wasn't anything there.

Iris continued, talking about how one day we were going to meet men who deserved our greatness and I agreed, keeping my responses minimal as I shared the elevator to the lobby with a half-dozen other people.

Luckily the line for Starbucks wasn't long.

"How's dingbat?" I asked after ordering for Mr. Devereux and myself. It was a bit of a gamble, getting a coffee for him and not making it myself, but I'd learned his exact order and made sure to taste that it was correct before I handed it over.

"Eh, dingbatty as usual. He's got a girl now."

"Seriously?" Our brother, Briar, was a lady's man, so to hear him settle on one girl for more than a couple of dates was astounding.

"Yeah. It's been like a month. When was the last time you talked to him?"

Too long. "Over a month ago."

She began to describe the girl in question as I entered the elevator, but between the interrupted connection and all the people talking, I only understood the words *leggy* and *blonde*.

"Sounds like his type," I replied as I stepped toward the large glass doors that led to Mr. Devereux's office. The doors opened to a waiting area, my L-shaped hardwood desk, and the intern's smaller desk across the space. There was a door that led to a small break-room area and kitchenette that held the over-the-top espresso machine that you needed a mechanical degree to operate. The room also held a door to a powder room, all to ensure that I was never far from my desk.

"Totally, but she's also different. I like her."

I set my purse and coffee down, freeing my hands so that I could unlock the door leading to Mr. Devereux's office. "Good. Maybe she's what he needs."

Between my desk and the intern's desk was a large wooden door that led to Mr. Devereux's office. Inside was another great space with a large executive desk with two large monitors. A flat-screen TV was mounted on the wall with two modern-style leather arm chairs and matching love-seat for sharing information. A rectangular, black mahogany table with a center glass stripe that sat up to six was on the opposite side, along with a set of built-in bookcases, a buffet, and a door that led to a full private bathroom. The corner office was framed by floor-to-ceiling windows.

The space was very masculine with few personal items— no warmth at all.

"Maybe." I stepped in and was nearly blinded by the morning sun shining.

With a touch of the screen next to his door the Roman shades dropped, diffusing the intense light. There was another set of shades that blocked out all light, at the touch of a screen. Much like the company, his office was state-of-the-art.

"You should come visit me," I said, as I sat Mr. Devereaux's coffee down and straightened his desk.

"You could visit me, too."

"Brat, I was just there for two weeks."

"That was *months* ago," she whined.

"Yeah, well, it's been two years since you last came out. You haven't even seen my new apartment." I walked back out to my desk and woke my computer up.

"It's a studio. Seen one, seen them all."

"Not true."

She gave a huff before letting out a long winded, "Fiiinnneee."

"Stop being a brat."

"But it's so wet there." I could hear the pout in her voice.

I took a sip of my coffee and let out a little moan as the warmth spread through me. Coffee was life. "We can do that underground tour and the Ferris wheel on the pier."

"We can't just hang?"

I rolled my eyes at my sister's lack of adventure. "It's fun, Iris."

"Okay, but I also want to see this new place and your new boss. The last one was sleazy as fuck. I had to steam clean my ass after he touched me."

Dante had flirted with Iris, thinking she was me, and she played along until she realized he was the man I talked about.

In my periphery, a figure headed through the glass doors, but it wasn't Stacey, the intern.

"Delivery," a portly man in a grey uniform with a red jacket said.

I stared at the delivery man, at the dozen red roses in his hand, and glanced at the clock. A bit early for any sort of delivery, especially since Mr. Devereux hadn't even arrived. It was also odd for a man to receive flowers, but not unheard of.

"Iris, I need to go. Find a date and let me know."

"Okie. Later," she called.

"Are you Ivy Prescot?" the man asked.

I nodded, and my brow furrowed. "Yes."

"For you," he said, as he set them down in front of me.

"Thank you." I stared down at the bouquet, not even noticing the man had left until I heard the click of the door.

A smile crept onto my face as I leaned down to smell the

flowers. In the center sat a card with my name written in elegant script.

> *Dearest Ivy,*
> *The best of luck to you on your new endeavor. Take no prisoners.*
> *Sincerely,*
> *Mike Deacon*

"Where did those come from?"

I jumped and looked up to find Mr. Devereux standing next to my desk, his eyes on the envelope in my hand.

"Boyfriend?"

"Hi, and no."

He quirked his brow and gestured to the flowers.

"They're from Mike Deacon."

"Mike Deacon from Chandelier?"

"Yes."

I was lost watching the way his fingers gently ran across the soft petals, wondering how they would feel against my skin. "Interesting that he would send you flowers."

"When I worked at Kilgore we were trying to obtain his account."

"Are you fucking him?" he asked, making all fantasy of his touch stop immediately.

Ah, there it was. That direct, almost accusing tone. It always set me on edge, like we were about to fight. "Excuse me?"

"Answer the question."

Why was it that nearly everything out of his mouth sounded like an accusation? It was getting old, and it all stemmed back to us not knowing each other. "Absolutely not."

"Then why is he sending you roses?"

"Not that I need to explain to you, but it's because we became friends, and he was just as excited as I was to get away from Dante."

"Hmph."

The vein jumped on my forehead. "I'm beginning to think the grass wasn't greener."

His eyes narrowed on me. "What did you say?"

"You heard me." I wasn't about to kowtow to him.

His jaw ticked, and he turned to walk away. "I'm your boss, Miss Prescot. My job is to run this company, not to make sure your precious feelings are taken care of."

"That's obvious." I knew he heard me, but he kept on walking.

Still, I wasn't going to let his soured mood affect mine. There was the small question of why Mike had sent them to me—a romantic gesture or a grand one?

CHAPTER 4

Lincoln

THE MORNINGS WERE ALWAYS A JUMPING-OFF POINT. THE to-do list was twenty lines deep before I even finished breakfast, which was delivered. Truth was, I had a gourmet kitchen and no time or inclination to use it. Good thing I lived in the city with a slew of restaurants to choose from.

The day started off with a spinach and goat cheese omelet and thick-cut wheat toast. It was the standard, delivered promptly every morning at six, unless I changed the menu for whatever reason.

At seven, my driver Austin, arrived, and we tackled the intense traffic. The office wasn't far, but the number of cars on the road made it impossible to make it there in under half an hour. Instead of driving the distance myself, Austin took care of it, giving me those precious moments to work.

I'd already finished up a report, gone through my email, and replied to a handful of messages by the time we pulled up to the Columbia Center.

"Thank you, Austin," I said as I exited the car.

"Have a good day, Mr. Devereux."

When I arrived at the fifty-first floor there was an obvious issue—Miss Prescot was missing. Being that it was nearly eight, it was a surprise for the door to be locked. Since her first day she was already moving the day along before I arrived, just how I liked it. That was weeks ago, and never a hiccup. An itch started in my chest but I couldn't identify it.

With each second that passed in which she was not in the office, my irritation grew. By the time she arrived, it was nearly half past eight, and the cup in her hand was not enough to still my ire. Because when relief washed over me at the sight of her, I knew that I'd been worried about her.

"You're late," I said without looking up as she set my morning coffee on my desk.

"I'm so sorry, sir. Traffic—"

"Is always a standstill. Leave earlier."

"Very good advice."

I glanced up from the document I was reading, barely catching a glimpse of the twitch in her jaw and the forced smile.

"Yes?" I ground out.

"What?"

"You're still standing there and you're obviously biting your tongue. Spit it out." It was a trait of hers that was getting on my nerves, especially since I knew she didn't have a problem speaking her mind.

"I can't believe you are behaving like this."

"I run on schedule, Miss Prescot. Every second of my day is planned out."

"A plan that I orchestrate."

"And every minute is money."

"Are you that money hungry?" she asked.

I looked up at her, wondering what she was playing at. "You are already on my bad side for the day—do you want to continue with this avenue?" I asked, tired of this conversation. "You're my assistant. Your job is to do anything I assign and to be here ready and waiting for me."

"I'm your assistant, not your slave."

"You are the modern equivalent. The only difference is that I pay you."

"Payment doesn't make it right."

"If you don't want to work for me, there's the door." I threw my hand out in the direction of the opening. "I was frank with you from the beginning—I'm not easy to work for. Do you understand now?"

"Oh, I have since day one."

"Good. Get out."

I couldn't stop myself from watching as she stomped away from me. Her ass—I wanted to grab it, bite it, watch it jiggle as I slammed into her.

Having her as my assistant had turned out to be a terrible idea. Every day I resisted the urge to spin her around, pin her to the wall or over my desk, and fuck her until the vibration in my veins calmed down.

I was irritable, and even more difficult. I took everything out on her, because she was the reason I was so worked up. To top it off, I still knew nothing of Dante's company.

It was confirmed that when she started with Dante in the early days of his company, her contract was of the most basic form. No foresight was given to someone of her position. No NDA, no non-compete clause—two things that were the first pages of her contract with me.

As I glanced at my calendar I took note of the new appointments that had been added. The one that stood out the most was the meeting with Chandelier. All it did was remind me that the CEO, Mike Deacon, sent Miss Prescot flowers earlier in the week, and how I hated the way my blood boiled with the thought of him wanting her.

"You built a relationship with Mike Deacon?" I asked later that day as she set down my afternoon coffee. We'd both cooled off, quite possibly due to finally getting some coffee in our systems.

While not intending to notice, I found that Miss Prescot was as much of a coffee addict as I was. We were both in a much better mood once we had at least one in our system.

"Yes. He's a gentleman."

I sat back in my chair and looked up at her, deciding if that was a jab at me or not. By the fire in her eyes, it was, but I let it go. "I'll need your help securing his account."

"Me?" she asked, but I could tell she wasn't surprised.

"He obviously cares for you, and I can use that."

For some reason, her stare unnerved me. Miss Prescot was more perceptive than she let on, and I had to be cautious and more calculating in my word choice. She wasn't one to blindly do whatever was asked of her, and she wasn't gullible in the least. In a way she reminded me a lot of her predecessor, Amanda, who had been with me for years.

"Can I ask you a question?" She laced her fingers together in front of her and shifted her weight to one leg. The movement caused her knee to pop out from her skirt. Just that little bit showed off the shapely lines of her legs, and the vision of them wrapped around my hips as I drilled into her flashed in front of my eyes.

I really needed to rein that shit in.

"It depends on the answer."

"Why did you hire me?"

Without falter or breaking eye contact, I told her nothing more than the truth. "You were the top candidate in a search that took more than a year."

"And because of what I know about Kilgore?"

I paused as I decided what way to go with my answer. If I said no, I'd be lying, something I refrained from doing, and I was certain she would catch on if she didn't already know. Of all things in the world to lie about, my contempt for Dante would not be one of them. "I won't lie, that was an enticing factor."

There was no explosion of anger or betrayal, only acceptance of what she probably already suspected. "There's no lost love between me and Dante. However, I also have moral standards."

Shit. "Meaning?"

"Meaning I will help you close the deal with Mike Deacon, not because it will burn Dante something fierce, but because I believe DCS to be the superior company and will treat Mike's account with the respect it demands. Pissing Dante off is just the icing on the cake."

Fuck. There it was—the wall. Getting anything out of her was going to be a chore. I was going to have to change my strategy, because simply acquiring his assistant as my own was presenting itself to be a dead end.

"How did you start working for Dante?" I asked, changing the topic away from what could end up a highly charged conversation. Between myself, Dante, and Mike, it was obvious her loyalty lay with Mike, and I needed to change that as soon as possible. *I* needed to be the one all of her attention was on.

For the first time in a very long time, I needed to earn someone's trust. Someone's trust that I knew I was going to break for my own benefit.

"I was finishing up my last semester at Kelley School of Business when I was approached by a headhunter who'd found my resume. The company was still in its infancy, and I was excited to help it grow. Only I thought I would advance in the company."

"And you didn't."

"No. I started out as second assistant and when he was done with her, I became the only assistant."

"Seriously?" What kind of fucked up system did he have going on? I knew he was a philanderer, but hiring women solely on the basis of fucking them was a waste of money and, sometimes, good employees.

"She was there to look pretty."

My brow furrowed, and I stood. Miss Prescot was such an unusual creature, and every response intrigued me more. "And you weren't?"

She didn't move back when I towered over her, or when I began to invade the bubble of personal space. I didn't stop the draw as it pulled me closer.

"Well, possibly. Only I wasn't just a pretty face."

"True."

Her eyes went wide, and she blinked at me while her hands relaxed to her side. "Wow."

"What?" I asked, confused by her obvious shock.

"Was that a compliment?"

I let out a low groan and stepped closer, our bodies inches apart. "Not only are you the most beautiful thing in this building, but one of the most intelligent. A deadly combination for a man like me."

Her breath hitched, skin flushed.

I traced her lips with my fingers, unable to deny the need to feel just how soft and plump they were.

Beautiful. Alluring. Sexy.

Fuckable.

It took all my strength to step away from her. To create a gap from the tension that generated when we were close together. Her blown pupils and pink cheeks were her tells. If I slid my hand up her skirt, I knew I'd find her wet and wanting. I'd already gone too far and I had to stop.

"Back to work, Miss Prescot."

"Yes, sir," she said in a whisper that was intoxicatingly breathy.

After she left, I stared at the door contemplating how to proceed. The only way for my plan to advance was with her knowledge. I needed something to open the gate, and she held the key. The question was—how far was I willing to go to get it?

CHAPTER 5

Ivy
Two weeks later

"MISS PRESCOT, GET IN HERE," MR. DEVEREUX'S VOICE growled into my ear.

There was not a second to respond before the click echoed in the receiver. I blew out a breath and stood, making sure to straighten out my skirt.

It was hard to believe over a month had passed in his presence. An entire month that I had managed not to murder him.

When I said I liked a challenge, I wasn't expecting the kind of demands and level of perfection he commanded. While I prided myself on those things, on being able to present that level of attention to detail, it never seemed to be enough.

During the interview I could have sworn he was flirting with me, or at least interested, but after my first week and the disastrous coffee incident, those thoughts went out the window.

Still, that didn't change the way my body reacted to even the sound of his voice. There was no denying that I was very attracted to him. Standing too close to him was to be avoided at all costs.

We may have been one to butt heads, but physically we were drawn to each other in ways I didn't understand.

He was on the phone when I stepped into his office. There was no acknowledgment, but I'd come to expect that, and so I waited.

As I stood there, I noticed that the lid was missing from his coffee cup and that it was empty. I immediately placed an order for a new one through the app and texted Stacey, the intern, to go pick it up. The man was insufferable when he was in a good mood, and I would do anything to keep away from his bad side. We were both coffee junkies, and keeping a full cup in front of him was a great pacifier.

Days weren't eight hours long, they were as long as Mr. Devereux was in the office, which was often over ten hours.

My feet hurt every day, my head was killing me, and I didn't have the energy to get undressed half the time when I got home—let alone be social. Unopened text messages filled my inbox, friends were ignored out of sheer exhaustion.

The weekends were my only period of rest, and I spent them like a hermit, safe in my shell made of fuzzy blankets recuperating. Along with all the chores that went along with being an adult, like grocery shopping and laundry. Almost two years prior, I managed to snag the cutest apartment near Pioneer Square. Sure, it was only a studio, but it was larger than my old one bedroom by almost double.

It was an end unit and had three walls of exposed common bond bricking, twelve-foot ceilings, large windows, a huge set of closets, and a stone-cladded bathroom with a large walk-in shower. I'd divided the space up into a living room by the way

I faced the sofa opposite the large shelving system that framed my television. The kitchen wasn't very big, but had stainless steel appliances and a butcher-block breakfast bar. Anytime I needed more counter space for cooking and prep I used the dining room table, which sat in the space between the kitchen and my bed. It was a large enough table that it handled multiple uses with ease, including Christmas cookie baking and decorating.

I made decent money with Dante, but even better with Mr. Devereux. For the first time, I was actually able to save a good chunk with every paycheck.

"Yes, sir?" I asked once he finished his call.

He threw a file down in front of me without even bothering to acknowledge me. "These are wrong. Fix them."

I picked up the file and thumbed through the pages. Three hours I'd spent collating all the information, nitpicking every single detail until it was perfection.

"How is it wrong?" I asked, my brow scrunched as I attempted to find an error.

"That's your problem to figure out."

I ground my teeth and counted to five. "How am I supposed to fix something I see no problem with if you won't tell me what the problem is?"

"I want it back in an hour and able to read it," he said, completely ignoring me.

"Perhaps you need glasses, sir," I shot back.

His eyes narrowed on me. "If I have trouble reading the information, our sixty-year-old client will."

"He'll be wearing his glasses, though, sir."

"Stop arguing and do it. Now, where's my lunch?"

"Right away."

I held my breath as I walked out and shut the door behind

me. Stacey stared at me from behind her desk, her eyes wide. My jaw was locked, and I stood there trying to reign my anger in.

"Can I help?" Stacey asked, her voice barely above a squeak.

For weeks I'd had trouble finding things for her to do, especially since I was still figuring out my own job, and I wasn't sure she was getting a true intern experience.

"Are you up to it?"

"Yes?" she replied tentatively, her face showing no signs of confidence.

"Yes?"

She nodded and with more strength behind it. "Yes."

I handed her the file. "I don't know what's wrong, but he says there's something wrong. Also, make it bigger."

She took the file and eagerly dug in while I picked up the phone and dialed Alex.

"Hi, how's your day?" she asked as soon as she picked up.

"I need a break, badly."

"That new little pastry shop was calling my name," she said, not even taking a second to think on it. "Want to check it out?"

"Perfect. I'll pick you up on my way down." After she confirmed, I turned back to Stacey. "I'll be back in a few minutes. If he asks, I'm changing my tampon."

Her eyes popped wide. "Why would you say that?"

"Men hate period talk. He'll go away real fast." A quick grab of my wallet, and I was out.

When the elevator doors opened on the forty-eighth floor, Alex stood there with her ever cheerful smile.

"Can I bottle your spirit?" I asked as she stepped on.

The cutest giggle came out of her mouth. "My

mother-in-law has been saying that for years."

"Are you just that happy?"

She shrugged. "I'm resilient and figure it's better to be positive than negative."

"I wish I had that outlook."

"Well, you are the assistant to Lincoln Devereux. I'm sure he's beaten down some of your shine."

I nodded in agreement. "I think so."

The elevator doors opened and we stepped out almost right in front of the new bakery that had just opened. The smell of freshly baked pastries assaulted us before we even reached their door. Somehow just the simple flavor in my senses was calming. Maybe a nice big bag of pastries would help.

"Oh, that smells so good," Alex said with a dreamy look on her face and a sigh.

A few minutes away with her was exactly what I needed. "You really like pastries, don't you?"

"This place will be my downfall." She began dreamily walking around, oohing and ahhing about all the different products they offered.

"Is there a favorite?"

She shook her head. "The mister always knows that when I'm mad at him, all he has to do is pick up a fresh baguette or a fluffy cream puff or croissant or a tart—really anything—and all is forgiven."

"Wait, you get mad?"

Another giggle. "Sometimes. So, what's going on upstairs?"

I blew out a breath. "I don't understand him. I'm trying so hard, but he's hot and cold and he puts this barrier up and it drives me crazy. This isn't what I signed up for."

"It's been, like, six weeks?"

I nodded. "Six very exhausting weeks."

"You're still in that adjustment period. From what I can tell, you both have strong personalities, so chances are you're going to butt heads. Give it some more time. Things will get better."

My lips formed a thin line, and I resigned myself to her being right. We were still in that "newlywed" phase, still trying to get to know one another. Maybe it was because I figured out Dante right away, but Lincoln Devereux wasn't so easy.

I picked up a small assortment of treats for Stacey, including a very yummy Nutella pinwheel that I was lucky to snag a sampling of—my way of saying thank you for letting me escape for a few minutes. I also grabbed one for me and a couple of croissants for the morning.

"Have a good rest of your day," I said as we rode the elevator back up.

"You, too. I hope the day gets better." The elevators slowed and she popped the last bite of the cookie she was munching into her mouth. "Let me know if you want to grab a drink tonight. Mister is out with the guys to a Mariners game tonight."

"A drink sounds perfect after this day." Or ten. Sadly, it wasn't a Friday when I could indulge, but one or two drinks would take the edge off.

"Yay!" The doors slid open and she stepped out. "Let me know what time you'll be out. We can check out that martini bar down the street."

"Will do," I said as I gave her a wave.

Only twenty minutes had passed since I left, but it felt like hours. A truly refreshing break.

Stacey was still working on the report, and I noticed a bag sitting on my desk.

"They just delivered it," she said as I looked through the containers to make sure they were correct.

"Good, because I honestly forgot about it." He had me so worked up I'd forgotten I ordered his lunch or that he was wanting it.

"I didn't tell him..." she trailed off, her body stiff as she looked at the door.

"Don't worry, it's fine." I set the box down in front of her. "I brought you back a treat."

Her mouth popped open as she looked down. "Ivy, you didn't have to."

I nodded. "Yes, I did. Enjoy."

A big smile lit up her face. "Thank you so much. Really." She stood and removed something from the printer and held it out. "It's all fixed."

"What was it?"

She went over the issue, and I noticed my ire had notched itself back up. I thanked her, grabbed his lunch, and entered his office.

"Here's the new file," I said as I held it out for him. He took it, giving me the opportunity to set the box down. "And here's your lunch."

He took it from me and scanned it over. "Better."

"Question."

"Hmm."

"Did you have to be so nasty about it?" I asked, my arms folded in front of me.

"It wasn't right."

"There was one number off of the calculation *you* gave me."

He looked up from the report. "Which one?"

I pointed to the line in the graph, then back up to the numbers. "That one. The numbers were transposed."

There was a pause as he looked them over. "Thank you."

"What was that?" I asked, needing to make sure I'd heard him correctly. In all the time I'd worked for him I'd barely gotten a word of praise, and it astounded me that the word rolled off his tongue so effortlessly.

"Thank you for finding my error, and forgive me for losing my temper."

I regarded him for a minute, trying to determine his level of sincerity. He looked truly contrite. "I forgive you. Now all you have to do is thank Stacey. She's the one who figured out what happened."

His brow scrunched. "Who is Stacey?"

I stared at him for a moment before I shook my head and sighed. Only the girl who has been sitting across from me for a month. "The intern."

"There's an intern?" he asked. Just when I was about to go off, his lip twitched up into a sexy little smirk.

"You're an asshole," I said without thinking. My blood froze for a second as I waited for his response.

He chuckled, which surprised me. "Oh, yes, that's why I hired you."

Maybe Alex was right. Maybe we just needed a little more time to get to know one another.

Time would tell.

CHAPTER 6

Lincoln

MISS PRESCOT WAS BETTER THAN I ANTICIPATED. IN JUST over two months, she managed to get ahead of my requests. A quick learner, she did her best to get everything perfect. For the most part, everything was perfect, and I was impressed. However, there were times that she was on the receiving end of my wrath.

I knew the fault was mine. Between my attraction to her and the walls I created, I'd given her little to work with. I knew it, but I continued to do it.

I was more and more enamored with her every day and had done my best to throw her off that, though I knew I failed more than once. Sending fake gifts to women I dated in the past seemed like a good idea, fake lunches with them, all to dissuade her from an interest in me. I knew she had a boyfriend, but the more obstacles between us, the better.

I even made her pick out the gifts to women she thought I was fucking.

"I need you to select a gift and send it to this address," I said as I handed her a slip of paper.

"What kind of gift?"

"For a woman." I studied her closely, noticed the way her jaw gave a slight tick.

"A girlfriend?"

"I don't have a girlfriend."

She looked up at me, her brow raised. *"But you're asking me to buy a gift for a woman."*

"Yes. I enjoyed the company of a beautiful woman for a few nights, that's all. I don't have the time or energy to devote to a relationship, but I do have a list of women who enjoy a night here and there."

I wasn't about to disclose that since her interview, I hadn't been able to think about being with any woman but her.

Still, I had her continue to set up lunch dates and buying gifts.

"You've got to be fucking kidding me, Linc," Dakota said over the phone. The fifth package had arrived. While the gifts were for different women, they all ended up at one of my little sister's storefronts.

"Just accept them," I said. She'd sent me a text with a "WTF?" after the first one, and I played it off as a mix up.

"Do you have any idea how weird it looks when you deliver this shit to one of my addresses?"

Dakota had three spa locations around the city and I never knew which one she was at, but it fit the story I was selling.

"Just accept them, Koa," I said, trying to sweeten it by calling her by the nickname I gave her when we were children.

"Don't Koa me. What the fuck is this all about?"

"Nothing you need to worry about. Give the stuff away to your employees. I don't give a shit what you do with it."

"Seriously, you fucking tell me right now."

I owed it to her, to tell her. She did follow me out to Seattle after… We both built lives after disaster leveled me. "It's a game, that's all."

"Trying to make some slut assistant jealous?"

I didn't appreciate her calling Ivy a slut, but I also wasn't forthcoming with what was going on. "Something like that."

"Fine. Could you send over some diamond earrings next time?"

I chuckled. "I'll see what I can do."

"Big ones, like a carat each."

I rolled my eyes. "Okay."

"And I want to actually attend one of these dates. You know, have lunch with my big brother who I haven't seen in months," she said, laying it on thick.

"I figured you were busy with Jack."

"Which reminds me, you are coming to the engagement party next month, aren't you?"

Fuck. I needed to make certain it was on my schedule and that I had a gift.

My little sister didn't just stay in Seattle for me, or at least after the first few years I was no longer the reason. Jack Ackerman, building contractor and amateur beer brewer, snagged her attention and last year popped the question. He was a great, down-to-earth guy and a perfect balance for Koa's energy.

"If I miss it, you will never forgive me," I said as I typed up a message for Miss Prescot.

"Damn straight."

"Lunch Wednesday?" I asked as I scanned my calendar.

"What if Wednesday doesn't work for me, Mr. CEO?"

I ignored her and sweetened it with the best Italian restaurant in town. "Angelos."

"That place is too pricey," she argued.

"I'm paying."

"I'll be there!"

I chuckled and shook my head. "Bye, Koa."

"Later, Linc."

I hung up the phone, a smile playing on my lips. Dakota was the breath I desperately needed.

"Is that a smile on your face, or are you just happy to see me?" Miss Prescot asked as she stepped in, a file and a cup of coffee in her hand.

"I was just catching up with my sister, but I am always happy to see you."

"Oh, I didn't know you had a sister," she said with surprise.

I nodded. "She's a pain, but I love her."

"Sisters are like that."

"Experience?"

She nodded. "But brothers are the worst."

I took a sip of the coffee and sighed. "That is exactly what I needed."

"You're going to turn into a coffee bean if you don't lay off a little."

I narrowed my eyes playfully at her. "And you should butt out and not try to break up me and my precious."

She let out a sweet giggle that I wished I could have recorded just to listen to it over and over.

"Are you going to hunch over and start stroking the cup? If so, I'm going to have to video it for prosperity."

"Are you trying to make me into one of those, what do they call it? Viral videos?"

She rolled her eyes. "I don't think many people would find it as funny as I do."

"Are you saying I'm not viral video material?"

"Not unless I made you into some angry music video about coffee."

"Coffee is life. I'm sure you'll be happy to spend some time with your boyfriend this weekend and away from me," I said. It was a desperate attempt to remind myself that the beauty before me was off limits in any other capacity than assisting me. Our conversation was making me forget, and I slipped when that happened.

"I don't have a boyfriend anymore," she admitted, and by her tone, I suspected it wasn't recent.

I froze for a fraction of a second and glanced at her while trying to not seem too interested. "What happened?"

"You."

My heart stopped dead in my chest. "Me? Is there something I should know?"

"Don't flatter yourself," she said as she typed on her phone. "Your insane hours are the cause. He broke up with me over voicemail."

"That seems harsh."

She shrugged. "We hadn't been together long, so it was kind of fitting."

"I was under the impression it was longer."

"It was only a few weeks, really," she admitted before changing the subject back to business. "Tomorrow you have lunch with Dan at one."

"Why so late?"

"It was all your schedules could afford this week."

I still remembered the day I was appointed CEO after less

than two years with the company. Dan was not happy to be passed up by a young newbie to the company, especially after working his way up through their ranks for a decade. He'd been CFO for less than a year, and still retained that title. There was some hostility in the beginning, but after a year, he changed his tune. I think the uptick of his paycheck helped with that. He also became what I would consider my only friend.

I had grown DCS so much that first year, but it paled to how the company grew the years following. What had once been a smaller data consolidation company had branched out drastically. Something that couldn't have been done without Dan working alongside me.

"You have a doctor's appointment in the morning, don't forget. I've already informed Austin. The doctor wants you to fast beforehand, so cancel tomorrow's breakfast or have it delivered here at a later time. Also, this is your last coffee of the day, no arguing."

The doctor was a necessary evil. I was on the verge of a few issues due to the stress of my job, and I knew he was going to bring them up again. The advice was always "Try to reduce your stress." Like that was an easy thing to do when you ran a hundred-million-dollar company.

I worked out, ate decently, in peak physical condition, and was healthy.

I glared up at her. "Excuse me?"

"Don't give me that look. You're not as scary as you think you are. And don't try to order Stacey to get it. I've also warned the Starbucks staff to not serve you, and Austin has been informed."

"Do you really think I'm that nefarious?"

"To get what you want? Absolutely."

She headed back to her desk and I pondered our conversation, wondering when we had become comfortable. Yes, I had my outbursts and demands, but the conversation had an ease I hadn't experienced since Amanda left. Small jabs, lighthearted comments, and playfulness.

And for fuck's sake, she giggled.

I definitely wanted to hear that again.

Due to the coffee restriction, I closed out our day at five instead of the usual schedule of staying late.

"Have a good evening, Miss Prescot," I said as the elevator doors opened onto the lobby.

"You, too, sir." She smiled at me, a true smile, and I smiled back, watching her as the doors closed, cutting us off.

At first, I'd wondered how she had worked for Dante for so long without succumbing to his advances and manipulations, but after a while it became obvious—Miss Prescot didn't put up with bullshit. She wasn't one to let people walk all over her without a fight. Submissive to a point, just enough to do her job, but more than that and she would put you in your place.

Ivy Prescot was born to sit next to a king as an equal ruler, not lay at the feet of a self-centered tyrant.

I stared through the glass windows to the grey sky and the ever-present dusting of dew that seemed to always be settled over the city. It made me miss Colorado and the wildly differing seasons, but I had to admit I didn't miss the frigid winters.

The lobby was packed with people heading out after the long day, a cacophony of voices echoing through the vast space.

Even through the myriad of sounds, one stood out. One

blood-boiling voice.

It'd been over a year since I'd seen him, but I would never be able to forget him or his voice. I resisted turning to the sound, but I couldn't help my need to fuel the fire that drove me. To look into the eyes of the man responsible for the tear in my chest.

To the man I was going to bury.

I couldn't kill him with my bare hands like I wanted to, so I was resigned to becoming the giant toppling his empire, crushing it and him beneath my shoe.

His dark eyes glanced up and caught mine for a fraction of a second. Then there was the spark of recognition, the double take.

A darkness rolled through me, eyes narrowing as my fists balled at my side. Time was never enough to still the staggering anger that consumed me. I still wanted to pummel his face, beat him until he was unrecognizable.

He bid farewell to whomever he was there to see, then headed toward me.

I should have left, continued on my path to the car, but I couldn't make my feet move in that direction.

"Lincoln, how good to see you again. How are you, old friend?" The smile that drew up on his face was done so with enough theatrics to convince the harshest of film critics.

He held out his hand, but all I could do was look down in disgust. "Don't call me that."

That sly smirk I'd seen so many times before surfaced, the one he wore as he repeated his innocence. "How do you like my leftovers?"

I shook my head. "She was never your leftovers."

"How do you know?"

"Because Miss Prescot is quite possibly the strongest woman I've ever met, and I don't for one second believe she'd ever let slime like you touch her."

"Resorting to name-calling already? I thought the hot shot CEO of DCS was more mature than this."

"Go crawl back to whatever girl you've convinced to love you with your bullshit lies."

"I've got a lot of those, but none were as good at sucking my dick as Lo—"

I snapped forward, cutting him off. "Don't you dare say her name," I snarled. "You never get to say her name. Ever." My whole body vibrated with the consuming need to lay him out on the marble floor.

"Jealous that she loved me more than you?"

"That could never happen."

"Of course not. I forgot how perfect Lincoln Devereux is. The world revolves around Lincoln Devereux."

"No, you narcissistic ass, the world revolves around you, remember? Isn't that what you made her believe?"

"She was weak, easy to lure away with a few sweet words and a promise of a life away from you."

I couldn't stop my reaction, stop myself from grabbing onto his collar without a care of who was watching.

"Once again you know nothing!" I spat out, teeth bared.

"No, it's you who knows nothing. You're blind, just like always. Trusting dipshit. I'll steal Ivy away, just like I did her."

I pushed off him and stepped back. "I'd like to see you fucking try."

"Mr. Devereux, do you need assistance?" Austin asked from behind me.

I enjoyed watching the way Dante's eyes widened, the

blood draining from his face at the behemoth of a man behind me. There was more than one reason I employed Austin. He was great for intimidation if the need ever arose.

"No. I'm done here." I turned and continued to the doors, Austin in step behind me.

"She has no loyalty to you, Lincoln," Dante yelled. "I can have her crawling back to me by the week's end!"

The anger crackled through me, blinding me, but I kept my goal in the front of my mind and kept walking.

I wasn't going to let him bait me into a fight. The pieces were falling into place, and my final strike would take him down.

Forgo a battle to win the war.

❧

Wet.

Red.

Pain.

Feelings and colors that coiled around me, drowning me. My chest felt like it was going to explode, and my eyes popped open as I drew in a harsh breath.

I rolled to the edge of the bed, frantic to breathe, to free myself from the crushing weight. My legs went out from under me, and I fell down to my hands and knees.

Breathe in.

Breathe out.

A flash of red.

In.

Out.

By the time my breathing regulated again, I was crumpled

all the way down to the floor. My vision was restored, but I still saw spots of red.

It had to have been more than four years since I'd had such an intense, grueling nightmare because I was in my old apartment, before I purchased the penthouse condo. Since then there had been dreams, but not the physically crushing nightmares. Those were a rarity after the first year.

I could still see it as I stared at the wall, because I had seen it. The vision was permanently burned into me, and my mind was cruel in making me relive it all again.

My chest felt like it was cracked open and spilling out, the pain somehow as fresh as the day my heart was ripped apart.

After a few minutes, I was able to get up and slowly make my way down to the kitchen. I needed a stiff drink to take the edge off. On my way down the hall, I touched each photo that hung, counting them, then I counted all that were on the living room wall until I reached the end at forty-two—the answer of my life, my universe, and me everything.

Because the brilliant smile of the woman in the photos was all of those.

The reason I was the way I was. The reason I was so driven.

I pulled the vodka from the fridge and poured about an inch worth into a glass, then threw it back. It burned all the way down, and I immediately chased it with another.

The nightmare had me on edge because of its sudden appearance. Was it because I'd run into Dante for the first time in over a year? That a part of me actually thought he could take Ivy away?

I poured another glass and tipped it back as I stared at the glowing numbers on the stove. It was just after two in the morning, and I wasn't sure if I was going to be able to get back to sleep, or if I even wanted to.

Every part of my body hurt, like I'd been punched repeatedly by a dozen men. I took another shot before padding over to the fireplace and turning it on. The sudden burst of the flame didn't even startle me, and I sat in the plush leather chair. I stared at the flames, at the orange and yellow as it danced behind the glass.

"Why?" I asked the air, but even I wasn't sure what it was about. All I knew was that everything felt fresh again. An open wound, making me a very angry animal.

CHAPTER 7

Ivy

THE TYRANT WAS BACK. I BLAMED THE DOCTOR'S appointment and lack of food and coffee. His mood was atrocious, and I'd come so close to smacking that sneer from his face.

I had so enjoyed our conversation the day before. For a few brief moments I actually liked him, but those seemed like a distant memory from long ago.

I wanted to get along with him. I wanted to get to know him, but he was making it impossible. Every time I thought we were finally headed to a good working relationship we took two steps back.

Or ten as the day would suggest.

Maybe a mile.

I even sent Stacey on some errands to save her from his ire.

"Did I not say I didn't want to be disturbed?" he growled when I entered.

"Yes, but I didn't think I was included."

"You are. Out."

My teeth ground together as anger flared. I was tired of being tossed out, ignored. How were we supposed to work together with his constant attitude? "What is wrong with you?"

"I don't want to be disturbed, and yet you are still standing here."

"I'm your assistant," I ground out, hating that he would even give me the courtesy of looking at me.

"And the biggest fucking distraction. Now get out."

I was done playing nice. "Why do you have to be such an ass?"

He turned and finally leveled that steely glare on me. "Why can't you follow the simplest of instructions?" he lashed out.

"Throwing me out of your office is not an instruction," I snapped back. "For weeks, I've been grinding hard to learn all I can, to understand you and how you work, but you make that almost an impossibility. You lock yourself away, won't open up or let me see how you work. How am I supposed to meet your expectations if I'm never given the opportunity to figure them out?"

I watched his fingers clench, then release, only to clench again.

"There is a reason for that."

"What reason?"

His entire body was coiled so tightly it felt like I was waiting for the inevitable snap. Had I pushed him too far?

"It's obviously your failure to understand, to connect. It's not my job to spell everything out, to tell you how to do things."

I stared at him in stunned silence. Somehow, I was being blamed for our lack of communication, for my inability to do my job. Not him or the lack of training. Me.

I had done so much to learn about him and his habits, to be able to anticipate his needs. Months of stowing away little bits of information and categorizing him just like the software he worked so hard to cultivate.

I wasn't the issue.

Anger boiled up. The tension that moved between us like a live wire only grew. We were at the end of the fuse, and I did not want to be looking for a new job when the dust settled. Something had to change.

But fuck it, I was mad.

I grabbed the nearest thing—a pen—and threw it at him. His brow furrowed as he looked down at the spot, then back to me.

"You're the issue, not me!" I cried out as I grabbed the next item. It bounced off him like the first, a completely unnoticeable hit. "I just want to help, to do my job, and you make that so *unbelievably* difficult!" The next item felt much heavier than the previous ones, but that didn't register until it was on its impact trajectory.

Time seemed to slow. His eyes went wide and he ducked before being struck. It wasn't until the item smashed into the wall, exploding into multiple pieces, that I knew what it was.

A stapler. *Shit!*

In two large steps he was able to reach out and grab me. I spun until I was sandwiched between the wall and a very angry Lincoln Devereux.

It was so different from the last time I was in his arms, but no less intoxicating.

His chest was pressed up against mine while I attempted to push away, but there was no way I was breaking through the wall on either side of me. My gaze was glued to his Adam's apple, and I could see the tick of his jaw.

"Miss Prescot, you are way out of line," he said in a low growl.

I shot my eyes up to his. "Me? Are you serious? Do you even register what you're doing right now?"

"You threw a stapler at my head," he seethed.

I glared at him. "I knew it would fly straighter than the file next to it."

His hands landed on my waist before slowly moving around to my back. The sound of my heart beating was deafening. The way my body burned under his touch, the way I desperately wanted to melt into him, was even stronger than the only other time his arms were around me. Turned on didn't come close to the feeling pulsing through me.

He leaned down, his mouth an inch from my ear. "You'll pay for that."

A shiver ran through me, and my fingers clenched the fabric of his suit.

Since I first bumped into him, I wondered what his lips felt like. Were they soft? Was he a sweet kisser or a taker?

I didn't have to wonder any longer, because no sooner had he finished his sentence then his lips crashed to mine.

Just as with his work, he demanded. Only a small squeak was able to pass as my mouth opened to him. Each swipe of his tongue against mine sent a spike of desire to my breasts and between my legs.

I drew in a breath as his palm flattened against my abdomen and slipped between my waistband and my skin. I tried to push him away, but all strength left me when the tips of his fingers grazed my clit.

His fingers slipped across my panties, a groan vibrated in

his chest, and his teeth nipped at my neck.

"Fuck, you're soaked."

I couldn't will myself to move. Every nerve was completely enraptured by him. My reaction was exactly why I kept my distance. Never had I felt lust with such intensity as in that moment, when I was in his arms.

A shuddered moan left me when his fingers flipped under the fabric and brushed directly against my clit. His hand moved down further, running against my slick folds, before slipping inside.

I drew in a breath, my mouth open as I stared into his lust-filled eyes.

"We shouldn't," I attempted to argue even as I clawed at him, needing him closer.

"We should. I know you want this," he said as he ground his palm against my clit and continued to finger me.

I tried to get my head back to level, to get us back to business, but my head was swimming, completely lost in the pleasure of his touch.

"Stop," I said in a breathy whisper.

A groan left me as his fingers slipped out, my hips flexed, chasing after him, needing him to continue.

"Why did you stop?"

"You say stop," he said, his body practically vibrating against mine. "I stop."

I was having trouble wrapping my mind around what he was saying. Yes, I said stop, but only in a weak plea that I knew I didn't mean. I wanted him even more after that, knowing I was safe in his hands.

"Don't stop," I said.

"Do you want to come?"

A whimper left me, my body begging for him to continue even as my mind feebly tried to convince me it was a bad idea. "Y-yes."

"This is all your fault," he said as his hand slipped back down.

My eyes rolled back as his fingers continued to work me, his lips and teeth nipping at my neck. A noise of protest left me even as my head fell back against the wall.

"I was being good, staying away from you, but you just won't stop." His touch became harder, hotter. It threatened to drag me away.

"It's my job."

He pressed his hand against mine, cupping the hard length beneath. When did I start rubbing him through his pants? My mouth began to salivate as he flexed into my touch. He was so incredibly hard and large, longer than my hand from my wrist to the tip of my middle finger by a few inches, and so thick I wasn't sure I'd be able to fully wrap my hand around him.

"This isn't part of your job."

I shook my head. "No."

"But you want it, just as badly as I do."

"Yes." It never occurred to me to offer anything short of the truth. Not in that moment when he was everything I wanted.

In a flurry of movement, suddenly I went from caressing him through his slacks to wrapping my hand around his incredibly hard shaft. The skin was hot to the touch but soft covering what felt like granite. His eyes closed, and a groan vibrated straight from his chest to my clit, making me gasp and jerk against his hand.

For a moment, our eyes locked as we touched each other. If felt like hours, reveling in an intense pleasure I'd never encountered before, but it was only a few seconds.

A whimper left me at the loss of one of his hands. "Open it," he said as he held a foil package in front of my lips.

A little niggle in the back of my mind tried to dissuade me from doing it, but opening the condom meant I could have him inside me, and him filling me was all I could think about.

Leaning slightly forward, I gripped the edge with my teeth, my gaze stuck on his, and jerked my head back, ripping it open. His breath was heavy as his lips ghosted mine, another soul devouring kiss before he swatted my hand away. After a pause, he then tugged my skirt up, panties still pulled to the side, and picked me up with ease, pressing me against the wall as he slid in.

Every nerve lit up, each hair standing on end as he filled me in a way no man had before. Stretched. Full.

Completely perfect.

"Fuck, so good," he groaned as he slid out, then slammed back in.

My body was pliant, bending to his every whim as it begged for harder, deeper. Don't stop.

Don't ever stop.

I couldn't think, could only feel each hard, fast thrust that drove me further and further to the edge. The pleasure spiked, making everything hotter as every muscle began to tighten until my breath hitched and snapped.

I cried out, my body spasming uncontrollably from waves of satisfaction that pulsed from the top of my head to my toes.

Somehow, he seemed to grow harder as he sped up, drawing out my orgasm before he stilled, crushing me between him and the wall, his cock twitching inside me as he let out a long, low groan.

His breath was hot against my neck as we both calmed down. It was also then the reality of what we had just done settled in.

He pulled back and when our eyes met, I could see the realization bloom in his as clarity returned. Not a word was said as he pulled out, though we both groaned at the loss.

The charged air was suddenly still and silent as he set me down. He guided me to his private bathroom where he stepped away for a moment as he disposed of the condom and buttoned his slacks back up.

My reflection showed a thoroughly fucked woman whose mind was completely blown because I hadn't even bothered to lower my skirt, and it was exactly who I was. I drew in a sharp breath at the feel of his hand between my legs, staring down as he fixed my panties, then my skirt.

All remained silent as he reached up and gently brushed his fingers through my hair, returning it to the tight bun it had previously been in before he knotted his fingers through it.

"That's pretty impressive," I said, noting the way he expertly twirled it back into position.

"Sisters."

"I take it the doctor's appointment didn't go so well?" I asked.

Our eyes met in the mirror, and he shook his head. "I was reprimanded for drinking half a bottle of vodka a few hours before."

I turned to him. "Why would you do that?"

"Ghosts."

My brow scrunched. "You were seeing ghosts?"

He shook his head. "Not in the physical sense."

With his words, I understood his mood, the desperation I

felt in his touch. He needed grounding, and the air around us ignited.

"Anything else, sir?" I asked awkwardly.

"That will be all, Miss Prescot," he said as he returned to his desk. It was like any other dismissal, like it was just another interruption.

But what else did I want? What happened was something unexpected and confusing.

Still, I could feel his eyes on me as I walked to the door. One glance back and our gazes met, his so intense it sent a shiver down my spine, my nipples tightened in response.

It was obvious neither of us were sure what just happened or what it meant. The atmosphere created an explosive environment, the culmination of weeks of tension.

I wasn't sure I was ready to go down that road.

CHAPTER 8

Lincoln

I DOWNED THE SHOT OF PATRON AND SLAMMED THE GLASS down on the bar top.

Shit.

I lost all control. All composure. I fucked my assistant. Rutted like a beast with no care in the world other than coming inside her, and it was better than any fantasy I'd dreamed up.

Another shot, then I fell down onto the sofa.

Nothing was going the way it was supposed to. Ivy gave nothing away about Dante, and the nightmares had returned. It wasn't every night, but even one left me reeling for days.

I'd hoped she'd open up, but then again, as she pointed out, I'd given her no reason to. Maybe I needed to change my strategy. No, no maybe. I needed to change, because keeping her away from me so I didn't fuck her obviously wasn't working. I'd had her and I wanted her again.

That was if she didn't quit and file a grievance against me. While I didn't believe she would, it was still a nagging feeling in my gut, which required another shot to help settle.

How was I going to get what I needed from her when there was now something I wanted equally as badly?

⬦

The next morning, I was repentant when I arrived at the office, ready to grovel if need be. The way I behaved was unacceptable, and I hoped she would forgive my transgression and continue working with me.

"Good morning, Mr. Devereux," Miss Prescot said as I stepped through the door.

She held a lidded cup in her outstretched hand. I stopped short and stared down at it.

"Is it poisonous?"

"Sir?" Her brow creased a tiny bit as she looked at me.

"Just wondering if I committed the ultimate sin yesterday and had to pay the price."

Her head tilted to the side as she stared at me. "Yesterday was...something."

"Something good or bad?"

"Not bad, but I'm not sure good for us either."

I gave a curt nod and took the cup from her. "Agreed. What's on the agenda today?" I asked as I headed into my office.

"You have a meeting with Dan at eleven, then a lunch reservation at O'Shea's, followed by a meeting with Greg Daniels at two."

I set my laptop bag down and pulled my jacket off, hanging it in the closet. "Join me for lunch."

She looked back down to her phone then back up. "Today is Sara."

"Sara won't be there," I said, deciding it was time to come clean.

"Did she cancel?"

I shook my head. "I haven't seen Sara in over six months. Yvette in eight."

"But then why?"

"Because I wanted you to stay away from me. In the end it didn't work, so enough of the pretense."

I kept my eyes on her, watching for her reaction. Like usual, it wasn't what I thought it would be. She wasn't angry, but more of an inquisitive confusion filled her features.

"You lied to me about having sex with women to keep me away?"

"Yes."

I could almost see the gears working in those beautiful blues of hers. "Dante uses that to seem more desirable. I guess I thought that was what you were doing, too, but I can see now I was wrong."

"Good, because I'd hate to be associated with him in any way."

"Does this mean you are finally going to let me really know you?" Another head tilt.

That was my way in, but it was one of the most difficult things for me to do.

"As much as it pains me to say it, you were right. I have avoided you in order to avoid temptation, to make sure you felt safe in your workplace. To distance myself in your eyes from Dante."

I watched as tension slipped from her muscles, a small smile playing on her lips. "You don't have to worry about that. You are a very different man than him."

"Hopefully a better man." I had to be, otherwise everything I was doing was a waste. It sickened me to even think it, but wasn't I manipulating Ivy? Wasn't I using her?

"Obviously, otherwise you would have been hitting on me from the start of the interview."

"I very much did hit on you in the lobby," I said as I remembered how much I was looking forward to receiving her call. One that would never come.

"Yes, well, the interview hadn't started."

"I never did get to ask you what you did for Dante," I said, steering the conversation into an area I'd been desperate for information on but had failed to give her incentive to talk about.

"I was his PA."

"I understand that much, but details. Were the duties similar to your duties with me?"

"Some. He's not as coordinated and driven as you are."

"Too busy fucking his employees."

"Are you really one to say that?" she asked, bringing the conversation back to where I didn't want it to be.

I stopped and stared at her. "That was different."

"Really?" By the hard set of her expression, the only way past this conversation was through.

I hated that I was having to put so much of myself out there, but I reminded myself to do whatever it took.

"Yes, really. I'm not going to sit here and tell you I was horny and you were available, because that is not what it was. I'm fairly certain I've given you every sign of my attraction to you and hopefully did not make you uncomfortable with the few times I was unable to hold back. I wasn't looking to fuck you, but there you were, pissing me off and giving off every sign that you wanted it. I wasn't in the headspace to stop myself from giving in."

"How do you know I wanted it?"

"Because instead of pushing me away like you should have, you wrapped your arms around my neck, refusing to let me go." I smirked at her, loving the way her face lit up in horror, pink coloring her skin. I had a feeling she didn't remember how she pulled at me, how she grabbed my cock. "After a moment I did try to push you away, but you were the one who held fast and kissed deeper. How was I supposed to say no to that?"

"Easy. Call it a mistake and move on." Her words held a biting edge, but I felt there was more going on here than met the eye. Maybe she regretted it.

I knew I didn't. I would never regret it.

"Is that what Dante calls it?"

"No, he calls it part of the job."

I quirked a brow at her. "And still, you escaped?"

"Yes."

"I'm beginning to find that hard to believe."

Her jaw ticked. "I'm not lying."

"How do I know that?" I asked, though I knew she hadn't. However, it seemed like we needed to have things out, all of the speculation and unasked questions. To get everything out on the table before we could continue.

"Because Dante is a pig who thinks women are there to serve him in all capacities. The way he runs that place is despicable, and I wanted to work for a company, for a boss, that had integrity."

"I have integrity?" I asked, somewhat surprised.

"Yes. Because if you didn't, we wouldn't be having this conversation."

"Because you would have quit?"

"Because you would have tried to have sex with me again already."

"And how do you know I don't want to, that I'm not thinking about how much I want you laid out on my desk right now?"

"I don't. And if you are, there is still a difference."

"That is?"

"Expectation versus reality."

"I don't get it. I really want you riding me right now," I said, being nothing but truthful. Every second she stood so close, my control crumbled.

"That's an expectation," she said, and I could see it in her eyes. She was crumbling, too.

"That will be reality."

She took a step back in an attempt to create some space, some relief for what I knew we were both feeling. "Hmm, maybe there isn't a difference between you two."

I stepped forward, following her. "There is."

"What's that?" Her voice wavered, and all I wanted to do was silence her with my mouth.

"I've been inside you. I know how you like it deep and hard."

"That's not it at all," she said, but her voice was weak and her lips were parted.

"Perhaps, but you're thinking about it."

She stepped back, her eyes glued on the floor. I watched the way her chest expanded in deep breaths. When her head rose, there was a resolve that hadn't been there before. "I don't want a repeat."

"Excuse me?"

She held up her hand. "I'm not saying I didn't enjoy it, but I want to keep our relationship professional. Nothing else."

I leaned in close enough to breathe in her scent. "I don't believe you." Fuck, all I wanted to do was take her in my arms and have a repeat.

"You told me in my interview you weren't looking for sex with your assistant."

"Things change."

"Convenience?"

I grabbed hold of her jaw, my lips ghosting hers. "Un-fucking-deniable attraction."

There was lust swirling in her eyes, her body vibrating against mine, but a determination and resolve above all. "I just want to work for you. Can you respect that, or do I have to hand in my resignation?"

My eyes went wide, and I leaned back. She was serious. It wasn't some off-handed comment. I wasn't ready to lose her yet—there was still so much information I needed on Dante. That, and she really was good at her job.

I released her and stepped back. "I won't seek you out. You have my word."

She gave a nod and picked her tablet up. "Good, then let's continue on with the schedule."

Fuck.

Things were even more complicated than I'd imagined.

CHAPTER 9

Ivy
Two months later

I WAS A LIAR.

I told him I didn't want to have sex with him again, but it was the hardest fabrication to keep up. He had kept his promise, but I was having trouble keeping up my lie. Why? Because things changed after that day.

Every time his hand rested on my lower back, or he leaned in, or he whispered in my ear, I nearly lost it. Physically, I wanted him. Yes, he opened up, but there was still something he kept locked away. While my job had become smoother, and our working relationship more fluid, he still kept me at bay.

He wasn't easy to figure out like Dante. Lincoln was more complicated, driven, and still somewhat mysterious.

Another late night after another taxing day, but at least I was blessed with my favorite vision of him, which was also a curse. When he worked late, the polished appearance gave way to a disheveled look with his tie gone and sleeves rolled up, his hair on end from pulling at it—a nice parting sight on an exhausting hell-filled day.

"Lincoln Devereux's office," I said into the headset. It was odd to get calls after six, let alone seven, but it wasn't unheard of.

"Hello, Ivy."

I heaved a sigh. "Do I need to block this number as well, Dante?"

"You could just listen to my offer."

"I've listened to many of your offers over the years and you know what? Not one of them was the least bit appealing."

"Come back, baby. This place is a mess without you."

I rolled my eyes. "Call me baby one more time, and I'll file a sexual harassment charge against you."

"For calling you baby? That's fucking ridiculous."

"No, for your continued propositioning of me after I have said no for five years and your refusal to stop contacting me. I'm so close to filing a restraining order. Do I need to go that far?"

"I'll have you back, Ivy. Keep playing hard to get. We'll talk more about it later."

I sighed and ended the call while I sent another number off to security to be flagged. For some reason, Dante had begun contacting me again. It was easy to block the numbers from my cell phone, but I was getting tired of it.

My threats were a joke, complete fabrications that wouldn't hold up in any court, but he didn't know that because no woman turned down the great Dante Kilgore.

Cue eye roll.

It wasn't that he called a lot, but for the past two months he'd gotten some bug up his ass a couple of times a week. For some reason, he couldn't get it through his thick skull that I wasn't coming back. I had more loyalty to Lincoln in the past few months than I ever had in all the years I worked for Dante.

There simply was nothing to be loyal to, whereas Lincoln Devereux strived hard every day not just for himself, but for all of the employees at DCS. Sure, there were times when I wanted to choke the bad attitude from him, but even that waned as we found our flow.

There was a strong thought in the back of my mind that said the only reason Dante was trying so hard to get me back was to one-up Lincoln, and I wouldn't put it past him. I knew he didn't like Lincoln when I applied for the position, but I'd never known the reason why.

Once again, the difference in standards between the two was astounding. I had to ask myself why I wasted so much time with Kilgore.

Years of bonuses tied up in stock options were one reason to stay. The other reason was just trite, but I was comfortable. I knew my job, and it was easier to just shut down Dante's advances than it was to go through the trouble of a reference and interviews.

I didn't reach my breaking point until I had to knee one of the managers in the groin to push him off after he ignored the word "no."

I'd already been sending out my resume and had a few interviews while I filed a grievance against him with HR. Thankfully the manager seemed to take what he'd done to heart, but it was such a "boys club" and I was done being regarded as nothing more than a toy.

While I still stumbled with DCS and Mr. Devereux, I finally felt like I was where I was meant to be—appreciated and my opinions processed instead of thrown aside because I was a woman.

I felt stronger, no longer resigned to fighting to be a person, and that was all because of one man.

One man I wanted more and more every day, but I'd asked him to stay back.

And just like when I told him to stop, he stayed back. He respected me and my request, and our relationship didn't change because of one day when we let it all get to us. It did, however, show me what kind of man he was, and he earned my respect.

"Miss Prescot?" Mr. Devereux called from inside his office.

"Yes, sir?"

"It's late. Let's close up."

Finally!

I began to dream of takeout and a hot bath with some soothing candles. Maybe even takeout in the hot bath.

Could I get my TV in the bathroom too? Oh! My laptop. That was the answer.

"Are you coming, sir?" I asked from his doorway once I had closed up and grabbed my purse.

He was unfolding his sleeves, which made me sad, but his tie was still missing. Again, visions of ripping his shirt open filled my mind.

When he was in a bad mood, the vision morphed to me tying him to a chair and stuffing his tie into his mouth. Those hazel eyes would glare at me as he fought against the restraints.

"Austin is going to be a few minutes, so I'll be a minute. You go on. Have a good evening."

"You, too. Same time?"

"Same channel," he said with that sexy smirk.

Mr. Devereux in a good mood was always nice. He actually

had a sense of humor and could be sweet. Aggravated Mr. Devereux was a different and unwelcome beast that was around more than I wanted, but still less than before. Settling him was an almost impossible task, and I hadn't quite figured out how to handle him when he got into such a mood.

As I rode the elevator I pulled the pins from my hair and shook it out, letting the tension slip away. It was always the first step in my relaxation routine.

When I arrived in the subterranean parking garage, it was pretty empty with only a few sparse cars. At least I wasn't the last one out again, something that had happened more than once.

I was feeling light and free and happy, as I always was once on my way home. The day had been long, with ups and downs, though the downs outweighed the ups in the end. Mr. Devereux's mood had only gotten better after five, but before five I was putting out fires every five minutes. I almost threw my arms up once and let the fire take over. There was a glitch in one of the programs that was making all the data go haywire. Someone had put a number in the code where there shouldn't have been and it took most of the day for someone else to figure it out.

There was something off about my car as I walked up to it and the closer I got, the more I noticed the lack of air in the back tire.

I was feeling good, getting my zen on, and it was crushed.

"Shit motherfucking ugh!" I screamed before kicking the tire, which hurt more than I was expecting. After a very tiring twelve-hour day, it was the icing on my shit cake.

I unlocked the car simply so I could open the door and slam it shut as I let out a scream of frustration. How long would it be until I got home to my bathtub and takeout?

"Miss Prescot, are you all right?" Mr. Devereux's voice called out.

My eyes went wide at the sound of his steps on the concrete growing louder. He released me for the day, I was free. Suddenly I was trapped again.

"Fine. Just a flat tire. I'll call Triple A."

I expected him to turn back and go to where Austin was waiting for him, but he continued toward me.

"You forgot this." He held out my phone, and my eyes went wide. How could I have forgotten that? I'd probably left it on my desk in my rush to leave.

"Thank you. *Now* I can call Triple A."

I watched as he flipped his jacket off his shoulders and pulled it off.

"What are you doing?"

He set his jacket in the backseat of my car, then proceeded to roll up his sleeves once again. "I can't very well leave you alone. Not this late at night with nobody else around."

"What are you doing?"

The corner of his mouth drew up into a smirk. "You just asked that."

"Well, it was an apt question."

"It'll take an hour for them to arrive, and another half an hour to change the tire, or I can do it."

I scoffed at him. "You? You don't do anything by yourself," I said with a little more snark than intended.

"I'm going to ignore that comment." He opened the trunk and stared down. "Do you have enough shit back here?" He rifled around, pushing things back until he was able to reach the compartment that held the spare.

"You're going to get your suit dirty," I argued with him as I pulled things out of the way and tossed them in the backseat. I really just wanted him to go so I could call and bitch in my car to Iris while I waited for help.

A little *me* time.

"And I'll have you send it to the cleaners in the morning," he said as he pulled out the jack.

His suits were not off the rack, and I cringed when he got down on one knee. The pavement was going to hurt the fabric. Would he blame me for that?

I watched as he jacked up the car, then almost expertly loosened the lug nuts. He was a fit man, which was somewhat odd knowing what he ate daily and his long work hours. The muscles under his shirt flexed against the fabric, tightening and stretching. It was hypnotic to watch, making my visions of tearing that shirt off him come alive again.

"Where did you learn to do this?" I asked in an attempt to get myself back on track.

"I wasn't always an executive."

"What? Impossible."

He gave a chuckle. "I know, but it's true. Once upon a time I was a Colorado kid who spent his summers on a farm doing odd jobs, including changing a few tires that are much bigger than this one."

"You? A farm hand?"

"It was a hobby farm," he explained as he slammed his hand against the rubber to loosen the tire. "My aunt and uncle's house. My sister and I would go spend a few weeks with them. She loved the animals and spent time with them while I got my hands dirty. They didn't have a lot of machinery, but what they did have I loved to learn how it worked. Other than that, basically I mowed twenty of the acres and was told it was fun."

"Was it?"

He nodded. "It was. Oddly relaxing to be on a tractor, bouncing around while the sun beat down and music blasted in your ears."

When he was done, there was grease and dirt all over his hands, shirt, and slacks, not to mention the rubbed spot across his forehead.

"Why did you do that?" I asked as I took one of his hands in mine and began scrubbing it with some wet wipes.

"I'm never one to pass up a lady in distress."

"But you could have called someone to do it for you," I reminded him.

His lip twitched up into a small smile. "Yes, I could have, but sometimes I like to be reminded I have redeeming qualities above the number in my checkbook."

"Do you?"

"I changed your flat tire."

I shrugged. "I could have done it."

His eyes narrowed at me. "Stop trying to steal my thunder."

That had me laughing. "I'm not. I'm just saying, it wasn't like heart surgery or something."

"Is that what it takes to impress you? If so, it'll be a while."

Heat flooded my cheeks. "Offering to help was impressive enough."

He smiled at me, seemingly happy with my response. Silence took over as we stared at each other. The closeness was creating an intoxicating atmosphere.

It was exactly the thing I avoided at all costs. Add in the playfulness and the barriers seemed to drop entirely. The butterflies began to flutter in my stomach, growing stronger with each passing second.

He reached up and lightly pushed my hair back behind my ear. "Your hair is so beautiful down. Why do you always wear it up?"

His fingers trailed down my neck, landed on my clavicle, and continued to my shoulder, leaving a trail of fire behind them.

My breath hitched, and warmth spread through me. "It's wet from the shower and I don't have time in the morning to dry it, so I pull it back," I said, noticing my voice wasn't much above a whisper.

"Miss Prescot?" His hand rested on my hip, his fingers flexing.

"Yes?"

"I want—"

"Mr. Devereux, there you are." Austin's voice cut in, startling us both. "Miss Prescot," he said with a nod.

Lincoln stepped back and cleared his throat. "Miss Prescot needed help with a flat tire."

Austin nodded and looked at the car, seeing the spare was on. "Should I bring the car around?"

"Yes."

With a nod, Austin turned and headed back to wherever he'd parked.

"You were saying?" I asked as I unconsciously stepped closer.

He looked away from me as he retrieved his coat from the backseat. "Yes, I want you to drive home safely and get that tire replaced as soon as possible."

I knew that wasn't what he was going to say, but rather what he needed to say.

It was the first nice thing he'd done for me, and there was no hidden agenda that I could see. It wasn't a tactic to get information or into my bed. He was showing me that he cared, even if he didn't say it.

The Continental came around the corner and slowed as it approached.

"Have a good evening, Miss Prescot," Mr. Devereux said as he climbed into the backseat.

For the first time, I wanted him to stay. Visions of him holding me while he told me more stories about his childhood danced around my head.

Why did we have to be so complicated?

∽

The next morning, just before I was going to head out, my phone went off with a text. What was odd was that it was a text from Austin, Mr. Devereux's driver.

Downstairs—Austin

I threw on my jacket and grabbed my purse before heading out the door.

The jet-black Lincoln Continental sat at the bottom of the steps that led to my apartment. At the bumper stood a hulk of a man who was well over six foot as he had at least six inches over Mr. Devereux's six foot two, wearing a black suit. His hair was almost as black as his suit, which contrasted with the deep tan of his skin. I didn't know his heritage, but I wouldn't be surprised if his ancestry held some Samoan.

Over the past few months most of our interactions were via text, but there was the occasional business lunch. The few times I was with him I noticed the looks. Often they were looks of fear based solely on his sheer size, but as soon as he flashed a smile, it was like he was their best friend. Odd to see how people flocked to him. He never seemed to meet a stranger.

However, that part of his personality only came out when it was the two of us. He was usually toned down when Lincoln was around. All business with the boss.

"Austin, what's going on?"

"Mr. Devereux wanted to make sure you were able to get to work without incident."

I glanced over to my car, to the undersized spare with no idea when I was going to have time to get it replaced.

"It's okay. My car is fine. Go pick him up."

Austin held the door behind the driver's seat open. "He insisted, and if we don't get going, I'll be late, so please, don't get me in trouble, Miss Prescot."

"Oh, way to twist that knife," I said as I stepped forward.

The corner of his mouth twisted up as he helped me in. "Whatever I need to do to get you in."

"Shady, Austin. Very shady."

A deep laugh left him as he shut the door and climbed in.

"Do you think I can count this as part of my hours worked?" I asked as we headed out.

"Aren't you salaried?"

Damn.

I blew out a breath and sighed. "Yes, but I should get paid extra if my morning commute is shared with him. Especially when I haven't had my coffee yet."

"We might have a few minutes to stop and get some."

My gaze in the mirror narrowed on him. "I thought you said we were running behind."

"That was just to get you in the car."

I hit the back of the seat with my hand, the smack resonating the space and making him laugh. With a sigh, I relaxed back into the seat and watched the city go by.

"How long have you worked for him?" I asked. It was possibly the first time we'd spent any measurable time together without Mr. Devereux, and a good time to get to know him better.

"Around four years. Ever since he moved into the Madison Tower."

"You're on call, right?" I asked and he nodded. "What do you do all day?"

"I'm in some college courses for programming, so Mr. Devereux lets me use space in the office to do my homework." He pulled into the drive through lane of Black Spell Coffee and just the proximity of coffee perked me up. "There's also a gym nearby, and my daughter's school. I'm able to pick her up and take her home every day."

"I didn't know you had a daughter."

He nodded. "She lives with her mom. I have joint custody, but the weeknights don't work, so I have her every afternoon for a few hours and every other weekend."

"That's awesome that you can do that."

"It's all thanks to Mr. Devereux. He's very understanding."

"I find that surprising." I still remembered the last time I was five minutes late because one of the high floor elevators was stuck on the sixtieth floor creating a backup for the others.

"He's still breaking you in. Trust me, under that harsh exterior is a good man."

As much as I didn't want to admit it, I already knew that. My relationship with him was different than most people because we worked so tightly together.

"Do I have to be completely beaten down before I see this unicorn side of him?" I joked.

"Nah, you just gotta be loyal. He's got secrets, just like everybody else."

Secrets.

The word stuck in my head all through ordering and the drive to the Madison Tower, where Mr. Devereux lived. I thought back to past conversations, responses, and my haunted thoughts corresponded with Austin's secrets revelation. There was more going on with Lincoln Devereux than met the eye.

The Madison Tower was one of those luxury condo buildings that overlooked the Puget Sound and therefore were more expensive than they probably should have been. I had no doubt they were beautiful on the inside.

"Good morning," he said as he slid into the car.

"Good morning." I pointed to the cup in my hand. "This is mine. That," I pointed to the one in the cup holder, "is yours. Get drinking."

"Mornings are for coffee and silence?" he asked.

"Yes. Now, shush." I held my finger to my lips.

"Yes, ma'am."

"And thank you for sending Austin," I added.

"You're welcome."

We traveled in thankful silence. Austin had music on low, and I focused on that as I sipped my coffee. I glanced over to Mr. Devereux, tablet in his lap, phone in his hand, other hand on his cup.

Always so focused. Always working. So driven that I was beginning to get worried about him. Austin's words echoed in my mind.

In my experience, there were two things that drove

people—money and power. The odd thing was that in the time I worked for him, Mr. Devereux never came off that way. Yes, he strove for money and power, but it was never for himself, never to lord over others, like Dante did.

The purpose was a mystery.

"What's your secret?"

CHAPTER 10

Lincoln

EVERYTHING IN THE CAR SUDDENLY BECAME STILL, QUIET enough to hear a pin drop.

"What?" I asked as I looked over to Miss Prescot. She was never afraid to ask questions or push my buttons, but by how wide her eyes were and how she was hiding behind the cup that was grasped tightly with both hands, she didn't mean to ask that one.

"Did I ask that out loud?"

"Yes."

Her eyes were wide as she stared at me like a frightened rabbit. "Oops."

I raised a brow at her. "Oops? That's all?"

She shrugged. "Well?"

I took a sip of my coffee, suddenly wishing there was some Baileys in it. "Everyone has secrets."

"True."

"Why do you want to know mine so badly?" I asked. She'd

managed to hit on an area I avoided. Not just with her, but with everyone.

"Because you are still a mystery to me, and I don't like that," she admitted. True, we were trying to be more transparent with one another, and it had greatly improved our working relationship, but there was still that side I kept to myself.

Some secrets could only be shared with time, and I wasn't ready to tell.

"What makes me a mystery?" Miss Prescot's mind always fascinated me, her candid nature even more so.

"Well, what drives you?"

I closed the tablet up in the case and turned a bit in the seat. "Power."

She shook her head. "No."

"No?"

"Well, yes, you want power, you strive for it, but that's not what drives you."

"And how do you know that?" I asked.

"Because your goal is selfish, but not self-centered."

My blood ran cold, flashes of red filling my vision. "How do you know my goal?" I asked, trying to keep my voice as calm and steady as I could. What had I given up that would lead her to that?

She shrugged and took a sip of her coffee. "I don't, but by your actions and how you do business, you're not...well, you're not like Dante."

I clenched and unclenched my jaw and as I looked over to her, really looked at her, I noticed her squirming a bit in her seat, still hiding behind her coffee cup.

"Thank you."

"Why do you hate him so much?" She slapped her hand

over her mouth and groaned. "See, this is why I don't talk to people before coffee. The mouth just says what the brain thinks, and its thoughts are basic and intrusive."

Once again, though invasive, I admired her candid nature. She didn't let much stand in her way in her quest to understand.

"I think we need to make this an everyday thing. It's quite entertaining," I said in an attempt to play things off, hoping she would end the line of questioning.

"What? My lack of filter?"

"Your reactions. To answer your question, Dante is a lying, manipulative, narcissistic bastard who deserves to be wallowing in the mud with the rest of the scum of the earth."

I watched as she tapped her perfectly manicured nail against her cup, her eyes studying me. She unnerved me sometimes, because she saw so much more than I wanted her to.

"Why do *you* hate him so much?" I asked. It was obvious from her interview and every day since that she despised him.

"Pretty much the same. Maybe one day you'll open up to how you found all that out."

"Maybe." And I would, but the outcome wouldn't be good for her. On that day, she would know everything about how I used her to take down the man who took everything from me.

❧

"Shit," I cursed under my breath as I rifled through my laptop bag with no success.

There was only a day left until my flight to Boston to visit my longest standing business relationship. Trips outside the office always put me on edge, always the itch in the back of my mind of what was I forgetting and what would explode while

I was away. It was better since Miss Prescot had worked out so well, and while I didn't do many trips, she was excellent in keeping me organized.

However, as I stared at my desk and my laptop bag, there was something missing.

"Miss Prescot," I said as I continued to shuffle through the stacks on my desk. I remembered her setting down a portfolio with all the statistics of the concierge report for Cameo International, along with the updates plan, but I couldn't find it.

Cameo was an account I brought to DCS. We had a long-standing relationship, and when I left Central Designs, Cameo came with me. Their account and the relationship I'd built with them was a milestone in my rise to CEO. Therefore, their portfolio would be much larger and noticeable on my desk.

"Why is my desk a pit?" Normally it was fairly clutter free, but in the days leading up to my absence, it had become a disaster. "Miss Prescot!"

Did she move it? I glanced to the door, expecting to see her step through, but she wasn't there.

"Miss Prescot!" I called out, and still no response. Irritation thumped through my veins and I stood, stomping to the door and throwing it open.

Her back was to me, but she didn't jump or anything.

"Damnit, Miss Prescot, are you suddenly deaf?"

No response.

"Ivy!"

I reached out and grabbed her arm, spinning her around. Her eyes popped wide, mouth dropping open.

"Hi," was all she said as I scowled down at her. "That's a sexy scowl you've got there."

"What the hell is going on? Why aren't you responding?"

She quirked a brow and smirked at me. "I'm not at your beck and call."

"Yes, you are. In fact, that is the definition of what a personal assistant does."

The sudden movement of her open hand tapping my forehead while she made a "Boop" sound had me blinking at her in confusion.

"Are you fucking drunk?" I asked. It was the only reasoning I could come up with for her strange behavior.

"Not in the least," she said with a smile.

"Then get your ass in my office," I growled. What kind of game was she playing?

"Was I a naughty girl? Are you going to spank me?" She bit down on her lower lip, her fingers sliding up and down my tie as she pulled.

I was so caught off guard that I failed to resist her drawing me nearer, her body bowing into mine. Something was off, but I couldn't put my finger on it. The energy was different and her eyes seemed the same, but off. The flecks of gold were in the wrong places. Her hair was down—when did she do that?

"Iris, let him go," Ivy's voice called.

It didn't come from the woman in front of me, and I turned to see Ivy standing a few feet from us. My head snapped back to the woman whose lips were inches from my own.

A smile broke out, and she began laughing as she let me go and stepped back, holding her stomach as she leaned over.

"Your face! Priceless!"

"I'm so sorry, sir," Ivy apologized.

"What is going on?" Was it one of those gotcha reality shows or something?

"This is my sister, Iris. She came in for the weekend. She was *supposed* to stay at my place." Ivy scowled at her doppelganger.

Iris gave a coy smile and shrugged. "I told you I wanted to see where you worked."

Ivy folded her arms in front of her. "And you snuck in using my face."

"It's my face, too," Iris argued.

"Well, here, it's mine."

I stared at the two of them, at the near identicalness of the women in front of me. Their banter, the way they played off each other. The familiarity struck me in the chest and it began to ache.

"You're a twin?" I asked, finally able to get a word in.

That caught Ivy's attention. "Yes. Iris lives in Indiana, and she came for a visit since I have a little time off."

Due to a combination of the many overtime hours Ivy clocked and my flight's earlier than normal departure, I had given her the time off while I was away. She wasn't completely off the hook, still on call, but I didn't think I'd need to call on her.

I held out my hand, keeping my distance as I was unsure what she would do. "It's a pleasure to meet you, Iris."

"Oh, the pleasure is definitely all mine," she said with a smile and a wink.

"Iris!" Ivy hissed before shooting me an apologetic look.

"Well, if you had mentioned it before, maybe I wouldn't have been so shell shocked," Iris said. Their eyes locked and they stared at each other for more than a few moments when Iris finally yelled out, "Fine!" and threw her hands in the air. "I'm sorry, Mr. Devereux. I think the jet lag is getting to me and I'm a bit loopy."

"Not a problem, just an odd surprise." I looked to Ivy. "Miss Prescot, I need you."

Iris made a noise, and Ivy shot her another glare. "Coming, sir."

Another noise from Iris and a "Stop it!" from Ivy. I couldn't help but chuckle, getting more enjoyment out of Iris's reaction to the double entendre than I intended.

"Yes, sir?"

"I can't find the Cameo portfolio."

"The CS report was missing the last weeks' worth of data, so I took it to be fixed," she said before running back to her desk. She was only gone a second, but it was enough for Iris to pop her head in and wink at me.

I let out a low chuckle and shook my head. Once I was over the shock, they were quite an entertaining duo.

Ivy ran back in, scowling at the doorway as she passed, and held out the portfolio. "Here you are. It has the most up-to-date information."

I leaned in close, and in a low voice asked her, "Why didn't you mention you were a twin?"

She blinked up at me. "Does it matter?"

Did it? No, but something about it struck me in a way I wasn't expecting. "It is an interesting Ivy fact. Who is older?"

"Me, by three minutes."

I glanced up at the clock, noting it was just after four. "How is everything looking? Are the preparations for Boston complete?"

"You're set now. Your flight leaves tomorrow at two. Austin will be here after your ten o'clock meeting with Techtonic."

"Good. Reservations at the Cameo Hotel?"

She nodded. "Yes, two nights in one of their suites."

"Good. Okay, I think we're set. Go on and head out for the day."

She stared at me. "Really?"

I had no idea her sister was coming in, or I might have given her more time off. Really, all she needed to do was ask. "I'll see you in the morning."

"Thank you, Mr. Devereux." She smiled up at me and bounced before throwing her arms around me.

I didn't even have enough time to get over my shock and wrap my arms around her, to catch her, when she released me and stepped back, her eyes wide. "I'm so sorry, sir."

My chest flared as I looked at her, desperate to have her where she was just seconds before.

"Have fun," I said as I tilted my head toward the door.

She smiled before nearly racing for the door like the dismissal bell had just rung.

I shook my head before sitting back down, listening to them giggle and Ivy handing phone duty to the intern.

I couldn't help but watch as she walked out the door, our eyes connecting for a fraction of a second as she glanced back.

The feel of her, the warmth, still lingered, and I missed it. I'd been good, but she continued to make it—and me—hard.

To make matters more interesting, Ivy was a twin.

Was that what drew me to her?

No, it wasn't. That was Ivy.

Not even her identical twin could affect me the same. Everything I felt was for Ivy alone.

CHAPTER 11

Ivy

"PLEASE, PLEASE, *PLEASE* TELL ME YOU ARE GETTING SOME of that man," Iris begged as we pulled up to my apartment.

I turned the car off and climbed out, hoping to get away from the conversation. For some reason I hadn't told Iris much about Lincoln, and I wasn't sure why. Maybe it was because I honestly didn't know what was going on between us and she had a tendency to want every single detail.

"He's my boss."

She climbed the stairs behind me. "Maybe, but he's divine."

"Yes, he is, but he's also an ass to work for."

"He has a fine one of those."

"What is with you?" I asked as I tossed my purse onto the table near the door.

She let out a sigh and fell down on my couch. "I don't know. Ever since things ended with Jeremy, I've had this itch I can't seem to scratch."

"Well, you're not using Mr. Devereux as your scratching post."

"Why haven't you told me?" she asked, her head tilted to the side.

"What?" I knew where she was going, and I wasn't sure how to respond to what was coming.

"That you slept with him. I can tell you have feelings for him."

I kicked my shoes off and fell down next to her, my head resting on her lap as I stared up at the ceiling. Her fingers threaded through my hair, and I unconsciously twirled one of her locks.

"I don't know what's going on," I replied.

"You like him."

"Yeah, and you're right, we've had sex. It's just…he's my boss. That complicates things."

"Was it good?" she asked.

"Very," I admitted. Try as I might, time didn't help me forget how good it was. I wanted him more and more, but was it for sex? A romantic relationship? Did he even do romance?

"But only once?"

"I told him I wanted a professional relationship."

She shook her head. "You are so full of shit."

I pursed my lips. "Yes, well, he doesn't know that."

"Are you sure? I saw the way he looked at you."

"Because you confused him by coming on to him while he thought you were me."

"And even then, he didn't look at me like he looked at you."

Really? I knew I shouldn't ask, but I couldn't stop myself. "How did he look at me?"

"Like there's this secret just between the two of you and

if you say anything about it, the world will end or something."

I stopped twirling her strand of hair. "That's kind of depressing."

"It's romantic."

"How so?" I asked. I'd missed Iris logic.

She sighed. "I'm not saying it right. It's just, he looks at you like he's got all these things stirring inside him, but he's stopped by this invisible wall." I could almost see the gears turning as she tried to remember whatever she was trying to clarify. "Longing! That's the word I was looking for."

I rolled my eyes. "Mr. Devereux doesn't long for me."

"How do you know?"

"It just…we can't…he's my boss, Iris!" It couldn't happen. I wasn't going to screw up a good thing.

"And? I don't get the issue here."

Of course she wouldn't, but then again, she'd never been an assistant before. She didn't know how close two people can become. In a way it came down to fear. I was afraid of ruining what we worked so hard to gain with something that could end up being nothing. I didn't want people to talk, to become that stereotypical boss/assistant relationship gossip fodder.

"I like working for him. I like working for DCS. It's so different from Kilgore, and I don't want to ruin that."

"Dad would like him."

I rolled my eyes, but was thankful for the subject change opportunity. "How is he? I talked to him last week and he seemed good."

"Butting heads with Briar like always." When wasn't that going on? It seemed like Briar lived just to argue with our father. "Dad started dating someone. Her name's Karen. She's nice."

"I heard a little about her. It's about time."

"Yeah. It's still weird to see him with someone else, you know?"

"I'm tired of him being lonely. He needs it."

Ever since Mom died, Dad worked hard to raise us. Three noisy, hormonal teenagers became his focus, and it always made me sad that he was missing companionship in his life, especially after we moved out.

"Besides, twelve years is enough," I said.

"Oh, she's not the first woman he's dated."

"I know, but she obviously is important if you met her." I knew he'd dated on and off for years, but they never turned into something serious enough to meet the kids. Karen had to be different.

"True."

I swung my legs around, flipping into a sitting position. "What are you hungry for?"

She quirked a brow at me. "Are you sure our twin thing isn't linked via our stomachs?"

"Fish and chips and beer?" I asked with a grin.

"Yes, please!"

⌒⌒

The next morning I drove in on my own for the second day in a row. Austin was taking Mr. Devereux to the airport after his morning meeting and I had the afternoon off. That way I could go back home to Iris. I'd gotten used to Austin at my door, a coffee run, and then Lincoln for the last week, and I wondered if that would continue upon his return.

I picked up two coffees from the lobby and headed up. Just as I was putting my things away and waking my computer up, the doors opened and Mr. Devereux strode through.

"Good morning, sir," I said with a smile as he walked in.

His eyes were glued to me as he closed the gap between us.

"Are you Ivy?" he asked.

I was a little taken back, but not entirely surprised after Iris's display the day before. "Of course. Do you really think I'd let my sister come here again?"

"With the way she was coming onto me, I'm not certain."

"She was playing with you. I'm so sorry about yesterday."

He grabbed my arm and turned me toward him, his fingers wrapping along my jaw, gently lifting my face toward his. I watched his eyes flit between my own before the tension left his grip and he let out a sigh.

"It really is you," he said.

"How do you know?" I asked. Most people had trouble, even those who knew us well.

"Your right eye. It has this gold stroke in your iris, toward the outer corner. Your sister doesn't have that."

Wow.

He was still touching me, his eyes locked on mine as his thumb swept across my bottom lip.

I tried not to be affected. Tried to ignore the way my lip burned from his touch, the way the heat soaked into my skin.

Maybe Iris was right, but I didn't know if I was willing to risk everything to see what might happen.

CHAPTER 12

Lincoln

BOSTON WEATHER WAS SHITTY—COLD AND RAINY, MAKING me thankful my time in the city was limited to two days.

I was meeting with one of my oldest clients from back in my developer days—Steven Hayes, CEO of Cameo International. Over more than a decade, I'd cultivated many of the systems that helped run the multi-billion-dollar company. At least in the background.

"I really wish you hadn't left writing systems and software."

"Why? Because I streamlined your company?"

He nodded. "It was a shame to lose your talent."

"You didn't lose it. You just have to pay more for it now."

He laughed at that. "True, but now I'm stuck working with developers who have half your ingenuity."

"You still have my product."

"And I love that it's always being revolutionized; however, it's just missing some of your genius. No matter what, I like doing business with you, and I'm glad to see you thriving at DCS."

"Thank you."

"But you need more than work in your life."

"Steven…" I trailed off, knowing exactly where the conversation was headed.

"Hear me out. For seven years you have skyrocketed DCS, made them the industry leader, but that's all you've done."

"I know how important family is to you." It was a conversation we'd had multiple times. A father of two, he was very family-oriented. His children weren't raised like the trust-fund babies they were. While his daughter became a powerful analyst, his son became a firefighter. And his daughter's husband was a firefighter.

"You should have someone by your side," he argued.

I shook my head. "I don't need anyone."

"That's the same thing Gavin said to me."

"Greyson?" I'd worked with Gavin Greyson on one or two occasions, but mostly with our secure cloud services.

He nodded. "Now he's leading Cates with a baby on the way and looking happier than ever."

"After that nasty divorce, I'm surprised he could even find happiness." I brought the glass of whiskey up to my lips and knocked it back before signaling to the bartender for another.

"It's always the last person you suspect: a subordinate, a hotel clerk, the woman sitting next to you on a flight."

"Right now, I'm—"

"Yes, yes, I know—focusing on work. Try not to lose yourself while trapped in all that work."

"I know who I am."

"Do you?"

I was a man with a mission. Revenge in my blood that begged for destruction. Some sort of retribution for the emptiness in my soul.

After that? It didn't matter. I didn't really care what happened after that. My goal was my only focus, no sense getting distracted by looking past the end game.

"I know why you strive so hard, but revenge won't bring her back. Get it, but don't forget to live while you do it."

"I'm so close," I said. Even Marcus confirmed it. Things were in motion.

"I know, and when you get there, promise me you'll take a sabbatical," he said as he pushed his chair back.

"What's that?" I asked in jest.

He smiled at me. "One of those long vacation things."

"Vacation? Who has time for that?"

"You will—once your mission is complete. You'll need a new mission, a new focus. Don't get lost. Find someone who grounds you, someone you can trust."

At his words, Ivy flashed in my mind. Her soft eyes and warm smile. My perfect storm.

"Easier said than done, my friend."

He held out his hand as he stood. "Lincoln, it was great seeing you again. As always, I can't wait to see what DCS does for us next."

"Say hi to Linda for me," I said as I shook his hand.

"Will do. Safe trip home tomorrow."

After Steven left, I sat at a booth in the hotel bar, working on another glass of whiskey while trying to not let my mind wander back to what Steven said.

Moreover, to whom his words made me think of.

Someone who made me feel, made my days better. Someone who I trusted more than I should.

"Hello, handsome," a sugar-coated voice said, as someone

slid into the open space across from me.

I looked over at the blonde in front of me. Overdone makeup, too much emphasis on her looks, and eyelashes she kept batting at me.

"Yes?"

"Just thought you'd like some company. You looked lonely over here by yourself." She played her seduction part fairly well. Her eyes were wide, lips slightly parted while she leaned forward to emphasize her breasts.

The show was almost sickening. I'd encountered more women like her than I could count. It was not appealing in the least.

"If you think letting me get my dick wet will get you something other than some banging sex, get the fuck away from me."

She blinked at me in confusion. "Excuse me."

"Did I stutter? If I want to fuck you, I'll come to you. Golddigging sluts who hang out in swanky hotel bars trying to find a sugar daddy aren't my thing."

Her face scrunched up and turned beet red before the inevitable tossing of her drink. It was a move I was familiar with, and I was able to duck away from the splash of liquid, a few drops landing on my suit regardless.

"Fucking asshole," she spat before stomping away.

"I never claimed to be anything else."

One of the wait staff was over in a flash, mopping up the liquid with a rag. "Mr. Devereux, I am so sorry. Let me get this cleaned up for you."

"Thank you—" I glanced down at the name tag "—Maggie." I gave her one of my killer smiles, enjoying the way she turned pink.

Maybe she was what I needed to help me get over this

obsession with Miss Prescot. It had been months with only my hand for company, trapped in a space every day with a woman I wanted but couldn't have. She was in my thoughts constantly, but she didn't want anything more than a professional relationship. Somehow, that bothered me.

Maggie left, but brought me a fresh drink a few minutes later.

Another drink or two and another hour later, I retreated to my room. It was late, but something bothered me, itching just below the surface of my skin, and drinking seemed like the best way to quiet it.

There was a bottle of whiskey on the wet bar, and I promptly opened it.

I hated the feeling that was taking over, the crawling across my nerves. The splashes of red that flashed across my vision.

I downed the first glass, trying to make the vision go away. My eyes squeezed tightly while I pleaded.

For years I'd managed to keep them down, push them away, but in recent weeks they kept attacking, leaving me on edge.

Without conscious thought, I heard Ivy's voice in my ear, and a quick glance at my hand revealed my phone and her name on the display. Somehow, I had called her.

"Mr. Devereux? What time is it?"

Time? I had no idea. I stared down at my phone, at the number in the right-hand corner. "Four in the morning."

"Sir, your flight is in…a few hours or something."

"Can I ask you a personal question?"

"Okay?" Her tone was dubious.

"Can a person come back from the edge?" Red flashed in my eyes. Deep and dark. Circling, covering, consuming.

Her voice was suddenly clearer. "Are you okay? What's wrong?"

"Can a person come back from the edge?" I asked again. I needed to know if I could have stopped it, if I could have saved her.

I wanted to know if, once I had my revenge, *I* could come back.

"What edge? Lincoln, what's going on?"

Lincoln.

Fuck, I loved the way my name rolled off her tongue.

I tapped the phone against my forehead. Why did I call her? I glanced down at the glass in my hand and found my answer.

"Forget it. I seem to have had too much to drink."

"Don't hang up. Talk to me." Her voice was frantic. Why was it frantic? I didn't want to talk anymore.

"Good night."

"Lincoln, wait."

"It's Mr. Devereux to you, Miss Prescot. Remember that," I growled into the receiver before hitting the end button and tossing my phone across the room.

It had barely settled when it began to ring incessantly. There was nothing to do but stare and wait for it to end, and it did, only to start up again.

I threw back the rest of my drink before standing from the couch and retrieving the phone from the ground. Immediately, I silenced the ringer.

When I awoke to the blaring of my alarm, my head felt like it was going to crack open. It was way too early, and I was fairly certain I was still drunk. The clock only showed an hour's difference from the last time I'd looked at it when I fallen onto the bed, proving the last part was probably correct.

Reluctantly, I looked at my phone and the nine missed phone calls along with a slew of text messages. There were also a few voicemails, but I didn't have the mind to process those.

Ivy's name covered the screen, and I clicked on the text messages.

Pick up the damn phone!—Prescot

Are you okay?—Prescot

You're an asshole to make me worry like this, you know?—Prescot

Do I need to do a wellness check?—Prescot

Text me back!—Prescot

Fuck. Last thing I needed was her acting out that threat. I typed a quick response before getting up and gathering my stuff. The driver was due in a few short minutes, and I needed to get going.

Fuck offf. I'l see yuo at airport—Devereux

It only took a few seconds for her to respond. **Drunken A S S H O L E—Prescot**

Two hours later I was seated in first class, starting the flight off with another drink before tilting the seat back, throwing on the blanket, and shutting my eyes.

The flight from Boston to Seattle was a long one. I was happy I only had to do it a few times a year. While I'd been able to get some decent sleep, I awoke to a splitting headache. Thankfully I didn't have any checked luggage and was able to head straight to the car waiting for me.

As I made my way through baggage claim, I nearly stopped in my tracks. Ivy stood, her hair down for the first time in weeks, looking so enticing. There was a pull to take her into my arms and find comfort in her body. It was hard to resist in my state, but I managed.

"Welcome back, Mr. Devereux," she said with a surprising smile.

I said nothing, but kept on walking. "Where's Austin?"

"He's waiting outside the doors."

Just outside stood the towering man in a black suit at the bumper of an equally black Lincoln Continental.

"Good morning, Mr. Devereux," Austin said as he reached for my bag.

"Morning."

"Sunglasses?" he asked.

I nodded, and he pulled out a pair from his coat pocket.

"Thank you," I said as I took them and pulled them on. The overcast sky was like knives stabbing my brain, and my eyes rejoiced in the dimming of the light.

"Does your head hurt?" Miss Prescot asked as she climbed in and slid over for me to climb in next.

"Yes."

"Good," she said before digging into her purse.

I turned and glared at her. "You're happy my head hurts?"

"Yes, after what you did last night." She poured a few pills into her palm, then held out her hand along with a bottle of water.

"What's that?"

"Something to help with your stupidity."

"Stupidity?"

"Getting so drunk you called your assistant in the middle of the night asking if people can come back from the edge? Yeah, stupid level of drinking had to occur."

I tossed the pills into my mouth and downed the entire bottle of water before sagging back into the seat and closing my eyes.

"I'm too old to drink that much."

"No, but you are old enough to know *how* to drink that much, and failed."

"What does that mean?"

"You didn't have any water probably. And no food for a while. Just kept drinking, I'm guessing."

"Guessing, or you called the hotel?"

"Both. A sweet guy named Caleb at the front desk confirmed my suspicion."

I let out a groan as the rustling of plastic rang in my ears. Austin handed a bag back to Ivy, who pulled out a Styrofoam container along with another bottle of water. When she opened the container, the smell of bacon filled my senses and my stomach gave a rumble.

"Bacon, breakfast potatoes, and a sausage and cheese sandwich," Ivy said as she prepared the container and fork.

"What's this?"

"Breakfast. Get something heavy in you to settle all the booze you poured in. Now, do you need me to feed it to you as well?"

I took the container from her. "I'm not an invalid."

"I was thinking child, but whatever," she shot back.

I glared at her as I took a bite of the sandwich. A couple of bites in, and my attitude changed. She was right, and I was already starting to feel better.

"Home or work, boss?" Austin asked as we finally made it out of SeaTac.

"Where else?" I countered.

"Well, considering you look like something the cat dragged in, I pushed your schedule back to the afternoon," Ivy said as she grabbed a potato from the container.

I wanted to argue with her, but my body was grateful for a break to recover.

"Thank you, but still, the office. I can rest there and get cleaned up."

She was taking far greater care of me than I deserved, and the ache in my chest as I looked at her grew even more.

∞

Days seemed to go by in a flash, a blink, and then gone. With that said, every time Miss Prescot entered my office, time seemed to slow. I couldn't help but look up when I heard her, watch the sway of her hips as she walked toward me.

It was the highlight of my day.

She was beautiful, and I hated that I couldn't touch her like I wanted to.

"Lunch is here," she said with a smile before placing the container in front of me.

I was so enamored with her that I didn't even notice what she set in front of me.

"What is this?" I asked in disdain as I stared down at the overabundance of green sprinkled with a few other colors.

"A salad."

I glared up at her. "Why?"

"Roughage, sir," she said before spinning around, giving me a view of that pert ass as she headed out.

I sighed and stared at the salad, my mouth turning down in disgust. As soon as the door clicked behind her, I picked up the phone and called her.

"Yes?" she answered.

"I want my sandwich from Othello's."

"Eat the salad, sir."

"Sandwich," I stressed.

"Salad," she said, matching my tone.

"Goddammit, Miss Prescot, get me the fucking sandwich."

"Enjoy your salad," she said, then hung up.

"Did she…" I stared at the phone before getting up, storming to the door, and throwing it open.

Miss Prescot jumped, as did the intern, whatever her name was.

"Sandwich," I growled.

"Salad."

I looked to the intern. "Call Othello's and get me the prime rib sandwich and fries."

"Y-yes, sir," she stammered as she began searching for their number.

"Don't touch the phone, Stacey."

"What is your problem?" I growled at Miss Prescot. "I'm your boss, remember. I tell you what to do, and you fucking do it."

"And your doctor said you need to cut back on the salt, and since I know you aren't eating well at home, you will be eating well at lunch."

"Fuck him."

"Stop being Mr. Grouchy. I'm not going to be responsible for you having a heart attack at thirty-six."

"My heart is fine," I argued. It really was. And the salt intake wasn't as big of a deal as she was making it out to be.

"But your blood pressure isn't."

"I wonder why? Maybe it's because someone thinks she can dictate conditions to me." My blood pressure was a little high—that was all. Stress induced.

She stood and stepped toward me. Heat poured through me at her touch, her hands resting on my chest, confusing me to no end, her body pressed to mine. Her gaze locked with mine as she moved her hands up my neck and then back down across my chest, her eyes wide, pink lips plump and so close. All it would take is a few small inches and I could have her lips, her tongue, then her pussy.

"Eat the salad. Please?" she said in a breathy whisper.

One small move, one sentence, and she completely disarmed me.

I blinked at her in stunned silence, my brow scrunched, mouth open.

Somehow a few minutes later I was sitting at my desk, choking down the salad as I pondered what had just happened.

CHAPTER 13

Ivy

I T WAS A DANGEROUS GAME I WAS PLAYING, BUT I FOUND IT was the only way to calm Mr. Devereux down when he was on a rampage. The confusion on his face the first time I did it was almost laughable if it wasn't for the fact that being so close, touching him, was like striking a match and setting off a blaze. Another minute, and we both would have been consumed and probably scarring Stacey for life.

In all my life, out of all the men I'd met, I had never had such a reaction to a man before. Even after months of working for him, the intensity was dizzying if I stayed close for too long.

Even Iris was calling me, begging me to just give in. At least that was her reasoning for her string of one-night stands—our twin connection made her do it.

I knew our connection was strong, but I wasn't so sure about taking the blame for her being horny. Then again, she was the reason my wrist ached for a month in college when she broke hers.

"I'm stuffed," Alex said as we loaded onto the elevator after lunch.

"It was your idea to eat six breadsticks *and* the entire bowl of pasta."

"But it was sooooo good."

I let out a laugh and shook my head. "You have a carb problem."

She blew out a breath. "I so do. They are my weakness. They're why I'm forty pounds overweight, but I don't care."

"You look great," I said with a smile and she beamed back at me.

"Thanks."

The car slowed down and lit up Alex's floor.

"Have a great rest of the day. Don't let your boss catch you hiding under your desk because you went into a carb coma."

The doors slid open. "A nap sounds divine right now. Good luck with the Chandelier pitch today," she said with a smile and a wave.

"Thanks," I managed to get out before the doors closed again.

The meeting between Chandelier and DCS was months in the making. Circumstances beyond anyone's control led to multiple meeting cancellations, but finally, after months of preparation and research, we were ready.

I knew Mike Deacon would be impressed with DCS just as I was, and I knew it was the support he needed to grow Chandelier the way he envisioned.

"Do you want me in there?" Stacey asked an hour later as she helped me arrange the portfolios around the table.

"It's going to be different from a lot of his other meetings," I said. She had been ghosting meetings for the last few months.

There was initiative in her, but it was hiding below her apprehensive exterior. Always eager to learn, her shyness often got in the way when it came to interaction.

"I could sit in the sofa chair and observe."

"That would be good."

She smiled at that, happy to be a part of things, but not at the same time. I often wondered once her internship was up what she was going to do.

I finished up a few small tasks while waiting for Mr. Devereux to return from a meeting on the forty-seventh floor. The sound of the large glass door opening caught my ear and I looked up, expecting to see Mr. Devereux, but instead the silver fox known as Mike Deacon strode through.

"Ivy, my dear, it's been too long," he said as he approached.

"Hi, Mike," I said with a smile as I stood to greet him.

He gave me that warm, blinding smile I remembered. "How are you?"

"Doing well. You?"

He took my hand and held it out as he looked me over. "You look well. DCS seems to be agreeing with you."

"More than Kilgore."

"Is Mr. Devereux part of that?" he asked.

I shook my head and rolled my eyes. "Mr. Devereux is definitely a different beast than Dante."

"Less sleazy?" he asked in a whisper.

"And more imposing," I said as I led him into Mr. Devereux's office. "Can I get you anything to drink? We have a gourmet coffee bar, water, soda, and really about anything you might want."

"Can that coffee bar make a latte?"

"Of course. Any flavoring?"

"Your sweetness is enough, but perhaps a splash of vanilla."

Heat flooded my face. Mike's flirtations were usually more subtle, and it was a bolder statement than I was used to.

"I'll be right back. Mr. Devereux should be in any moment."

I headed into the small break room, and began prepping the machine. It'd taken some getting used to in the beginning, and had given me a few good steam burns, but we'd come to an understanding. The fridge was thankfully normally stocked with milk for Mr. Devereux's coffee concoction.

I made one for the boss as well, because any time was coffee time for him. The man drank way too many of them. Then again, I wasn't one to talk. Every morning I picked one up on my trip to the office, and then when I arrived, I usually picked up another.

"Morning, Ivy," Dan called from the doorway.

"Morning, Mr. Stanton. Ready for the meeting?"

"Absolutely. Any chance I could get one of those?" he said, giving me his best attempt at a dazzling smile.

"I suppose I could," I said with a roll of my eyes. It was just for dramatic effect.

"How is his mood today?" he asked.

"It's Chandelier. He better be chipper."

"Then that better be strong," he said, pointing to the cups.

"Mike Deacon is already in there. Scoot."

"Yes, ma'am."

Once done, I loaded all three cups, plus one for myself, onto a small tray and headed out. I set it down on my desk to pick up my tablet and my phone, when I heard my name.

"Ivy is quite magnificent, isn't she?" I overhead Mike say.

It was a line that made me stop in my tracks, my heart thumping in my chest. Mr. Devereux must have returned while

I was busy with the drinks. The small seconds waiting for his response seemed to pass like hours.

"Yes, she is," Mr. Devereux replied. His tone was stiff, which was odd, because he'd been in a decent mood before he ran downstairs.

"He really lucked out," Dan said.

"May I ask if you know if she's dating anyone?" I heard Mike ask. It seemed an oddly personal thing to ask, especially at a business meeting.

"She's not available," Mr. Devereux snapped. My brow furrowed in confusion. Why would he say that?

"That wasn't what I was asking, Lincoln."

"I understood the question, Mike." There was an edge to his tone that confused me.

"She's very alluring. I completely understand," Mike said. His words made my face heat up.

"Understand what?" I knew that tone, Mr. Devereux was gearing up.

"Your possessiveness."

I thought I heard something like "the fuck" but I couldn't be sure because there was a sudden sound of movement, almost like a scuffle. Dan called out Mr. Devereux's name before I heard him growl, "What the hell, Lincoln? What is going on with you?"

There was silence, and I took that as my opportunity to head in while I tried to figure out why things had become so quiet.

"Coffee?" I asked as I stepped in.

Three sets of eyes turned to me, but only one caught my attention. Mr. Devereux's eyes held a fire, a blaze that sent a chill through me. I passed out the coffee and his fingers lingered against mine a little too long, and I looked to find him staring at me.

I didn't know what happened, but the air between us was charged and alight after months of simmering, of keeping it in check. My special way of calming him hadn't even approached the level that vibrated in the space between us.

After setting the tray down, I took my seat next to Mr. Devereux and looked around the table, noticing the awkward tension that filled the space between the three men. Dan's eyes were wide as he looked between Mr. Devereux and Mike before catching mine and mouthing something. I thought it was "what's going on" but I couldn't be sure, so I shrugged in response.

A couple of sips and Mr. Devereux began to relax, something that didn't go unnoticed by Mike, and the odd tension began to slip away.

"He's a bit of a coffee tyrant," Dan whispered across the table to Mike, who chuckled.

"Dan," Mr. Devereux said, narrowing his eyes.

"There's a reason I don't schedule any meetings with you before nine," Dan admitted as he took another sip.

"Hmm," was his response as he continued to drink. "Well, he's not exactly wrong."

Whatever had transpired was pushed back and replaced by a mutual appreciation for coffee. I heaved an internal sigh and mouthed "thank you" to Dan, who smiled. After years of working with Mr. Devereux, Dan had gained an understanding of not only his moods, but how to dispel them. I had my own tricks, but one thing was for certain—coffee made everything better.

"Coffee is quite magical," Mike said. "And this is quite good."

"What do you normally serve to clients?" Mr. Devereux asked, almost as a peace question.

"We have a few varieties, some dependent on the customer, but I don't think we have this."

"Black Spell Brew is exactly like their name. I don't exactly mean to endorse them because they are a client, but this coffee is really the best."

Mike raised his cup. "Agreed."

Coffee seemed to be the topic to smooth over whatever strife had taken over, and the meeting continued.

Watching him talk to Mike, Mr. Devereux was charming. While he wasn't an account salesman, he knew the products better than most CEOs. For larger accounts, such as Chandelier, he liked to handle their setup personally. That way he was able to tailor the experience and garner an understanding of their needs. After all, Chandelier was all about a tailored experience.

It was obvious Mr. Devereux liked delving into the customer's needs, because he got so animated as he talked about how to make new and different systems work. There was so much energy pouring out of him as he spoke, new ideas coming to him as he scribbled notes.

By Mike's surprised expression, he was sensing how DCS was run completely different than Kilgore.

"I'll be honest. I might not have considered DCS, especially after the way Dante spoke of you, Lincoln. He gave off a horrible impression," Mike confessed as the meeting wound down.

"That doesn't surprise me," Mr. Devereux said with a huff.

A smile grew on Mike's face. "However, after meeting you, I've determined that was out of fear. Dante is scared of you and DCS."

"As he should be. Especially me."

Mike nodded as he gathered up his things. "Ivy is why I came here today, but you are the reason I am leaving with the expectation of contracts to be delivered." Mike smiled at me. "I'm pleased to know you're in good hands, Ivy. However, if something ever changes, you have my number and I'll hope you'll call."

"Thank you, Mike," I said with a smile.

"Pleasure to meet you, Dan."

"Same. Looking forward to working with you," Dan replied.

"Take good care of her, Devereux," Mike said as he turned toward the door. "She's one in a million."

"I couldn't agree more," Mr. Devereux said, his hand moving to rest on my lower back.

The action shocked me, all of my attention suddenly focused on where his hand lay, on the heat that radiated into my skin. I tried not to act like it was a big deal, but it was, because he hadn't touched me in any way other that what was necessary or polite since I demanded propriety.

My heart tapped wildly in my chest. The tension that always sat below the surface began to vibrate between us, making my skin pebble and my nipples tighten.

With one last wave, Mike headed out the door.

"That was interesting," Dan said as soon as Mike disappeared. I managed to catch him glance at Mr. Devereux, and more specifically, noticing where his hand rested.

Mr. Devereux didn't seem to agree with Dan, his fingers flexing against me. "That was him pressing my buttons for fun."

I was beginning to wonder if that was what he was doing to me as heat pooled between my thighs. Much longer and I would need to run away before I did something I regretted, like spread my legs to him just to get some relief.

"Well, whatever it was, he knew just the nerve to strike," Dan said as he glanced over to me.

My brow furrowed and I caught Mr. Devereux's eye, but he quickly looked away.

"What?" I asked.

"Nothing." He held out a condensed sheet of the notes from their conversation to Dan. "Call legal, have them draw up the contracts with those specifications."

"Will do," Dan said before giving us one last look and heading down the hall back to his office.

We didn't move, still stuck, frozen, bound by the hand on my back that I desperately wanted between my thighs.

"I need another coffee," he managed to grind out, giving us a way to break the cycle of energy that trapped us.

"I'll be right back," I said as I pried myself away. The world seemed to dim when his hand disappeared from me.

When I made it out, Dan was at Stacey's desk talking something over.

"What was that all about?" I whispered to him.

"Turf wars."

"Turf wars?" I questioned.

"Ivy, you're smart, but you've put up blinders. Even Stacey here knows who the turf was."

I blinked at him, my heart hammering in my chest. I gave them a nod before moving into the kitchenette to make another coffee. While there I thought back at the conversation, of his reactions.

Months of keeping our distance, getting to know one another, keeping things professional, seemed to shatter the moment Mike came in. It only highlighted that the attraction was not only still there, but stronger than ever.

After a few steadying breaths and a fresh coffee, I stepped out. Dan was gone, and Stacey was back to trying to decipher Mr. Devereux's shorthand.

When I returned, he was staring at his monitors, his brow knitted, lips pressed into a thin line.

"What is it?" I asked as I set the coffee down next to him.

"I have that dinner next week, correct?"

I pulled up my phone and brought up the completely full calendar. "Yes. The Seattle Chamber of Commerce on Thursday at seven."

"I'd like you to accompany me."

"Sir?" I blinked at him. In the months I'd worked for him, he had never taken me with him for anything out of town or outside of business hours.

"It would be a great learning and networking experience for you. Also, I'm in need of a date."

"You could call up Yvette or Sara."

His head moved slowly around, his eyes narrowing at me. "I'm not sure I appreciate your humor."

I couldn't stop the laugh that erupted. "Oh, but I do."

He gave me a playful half grin. "Is that a yes, Miss Prescot?"

"If I'm your date, do I get to call you Lincoln?" I asked, not really thinking about the implications.

The playful scowl left his face and was replaced with a blaze in his eyes. "Do I get to call you Ivy?"

His voice was low, seductive, and it made me draw in a breath. He'd never called me by my first name, and suddenly I understood his reaction. In my life many men had called me by my first name, but not one of them had the same spine-tingling effect his voice created.

With the curtain of formality lowered, it also seemed to suppress the restrictions I'd set in place.

"You always could, sir." I forced myself to step away, to break the spell he cast on me. The spell that drew us closer and closer together. Two planets threatening to crash into each other that could end in mass destruction of everything.

CHAPTER 14

Ivy

"Wow," I said as I stared at my reflection in the mirror a few days later. When Mr. Devereux asked me to accompany him, I hadn't expected a black-tie affair. Thankfully, he'd had his personal shopper pick me up an outfit for the evening.

It was the quintessential little black dress. The fabric hugged my skin in all the right ways all the way to the ground, accentuating my curves. One shoulder was exposed, and a folded detail trailed up my other shoulder, almost looking like a tie.

It was every bit classy and elegant, and I was afraid to move in it. I saw the name on the tag, the name matching the one on his suit.

"You look stunning," Lincoln said as he stood next to my desk.

I was glued to the spot staring at him. He always looked good in a suit, but the Armani three-piece with its black-on-black pinstriping made him even more devastatingly handsome—if such a thing was possible.

"Wow."

His brow rose. "Wow?"

"I'm trying to figure out if there is any way you could wear that suit every day."

"I take it you like it."

"Understatement," I said in a low voice as I looked down to the dress and smoothed the fabric.

He pushed off the desk and moved to stand in front of me. The butterflies kicked up in my stomach with every inch he closed between us.

"I'll make you a deal. I'll wear this every day if you wear that."

"That sounds a little too personal."

"Personal?"

"I'm not sure I like you enough to risk getting this dirty," I teased.

When our eyes met, a wave of heat surged through me. He was close enough I could feel the warmth of his body, that familiar buzz on my skin from the energy that seemed to vibrate between us.

"Then perhaps you should take it off." His voice was lower than normal, and his hand rose to touch me but faltered, returning to his side.

"But then I'd only be in my undergarments."

"I'm failing to see the issue."

I bit my lip and shook my head. "You're being bad."

"Forgive me."

I reached up and straightened his tie. "Nothing to forgive."

The air was charged, and I'd already done the worst thing I could—I touched him.

Thankfully his phone began ringing, and he stepped back as he pulled it from his pocket.

"Yes. We're on our way." He ended the call and looked to me. "Austin is downstairs."

Lincoln held out his arm and I slipped mine through, trying to ignore the spark that passed as I did so.

The lobby was empty as we crossed the marble floors and out the main doors to Austin and the waiting Continental.

"Good evening, Austin," I said as he held the door open.

"Miss Prescot," he said with a smile and a nod.

With no traffic to hold us up, we made it to the dock in only a few minutes. Excitement buzzed as I stared out at the large yacht that would be the location of the evening's event.

Austin dropped us off at the end of the dock and once again, Lincoln held out his arm for me. There was a line of well-dressed men and women heading down, and I wrapped both arms around his when the wind whipped past.

"That's a big boat," I said, noticing the way it dwarfed the people walking up the gangway.

A chuckle vibrated in his chest while my mouth dropped open when we stepped on.

The yacht was huge. It had to surpass a hundred plus feet in length. Tables filled the bottom deck where dinner was to be while people filled the top. The space was a bit tight with the massive opening in the center that looked down to the main deck, a huge sparkling chandelier hung in the center.

The chatter was less of a hum and more of a roar. High-pitched laughter, names being shouted, and just general loud talking of people trying to hear each other over the music. In the sea of faces, there were one or two familiar ones but not many I could put names to.

Lincoln motioned toward a tall, black-haired man who was entertaining a group of people with what looked like one hell of a fish tale. "That over there is Will Montgomery. He's the owner of Black Spell Brew."

"Oh, wow." It was Lincoln's favorite coffee, and I knew they were the ones that gave him the elite machine in the kitchenette.

As we walked around, I was a little shocked at how many people he knew. For months I'd never seen him have a friend, yet he was friendly and engaging to nearly every person we saw. He knew their spouse's names, children's names, made non-committal dates for golf or lunch.

It was nice to see him in such a different atmosphere.

Hors d'oeuvres circled around on silver trays by waiters in white, making them stand out against the mostly black attire.

A few hours later, the heat, full stomach, and gentle rocking got to me, and I excused myself before heading up to the top deck for some air. There were a couple of people doing the same, one or two who were smoking, but it was fairly sparse, especially compared to the crowd below.

The city twinkled all around in various colors.

I gave a little laugh as I took in my evening. Cruising on a yacht drinking champagne around the Sound was not how I envisioned my Thursday evening. Especially since it was a work event with my boss.

However, it was quite possibly one of the most awesome experiences of the five years I'd lived in Seattle.

I stared out over the water, at the lights of the city, taking it all in. The air was cool against my skin, and a shiver rolled through me with each gust that blew by. The view was so beautiful that I wasn't about to let a little cold push me back inside.

A shudder left me, but suddenly my shoulders were covered with a warm jacket. Lincoln stepped up beside me and leaned into the banister, blocking the breeze.

"Thank you," I said, to which he smiled back.

"It's chilly out here."

"Yes, but you don't get as good of a view inside."

He nodded and looked out. We stood in silence, shoulder to shoulder, just taking everything in. The Space Needle grew closer and I stared up, trying to see if anyone was in the observatory staring back.

"I wonder what we look like from up there," he said.

I turned to him. "Not much different than from your office, I suppose, but it's still fun, especially the restaurant."

"Restaurant?"

"Yes, the spinning one."

"I didn't know there was one," he admitted.

I turned toward him. "You have been, haven't you?"

He shook his head. "No."

I blinked at him. "You've been here how long and never been to the Space Needle?"

He gave me a sheepish grin. "I've been a little busy."

"But not even taking an hour to go visit Seattle's greatest landmark?" I asked. He had to be messing with me. "I've been here five years and gone almost a dozen times."

"Good for you."

"Seriously, you need to. Do you have any plans this weekend?"

He made a small grunt. "Work."

I let out a huff. "That's it? Do you ever do anything besides work?"

"Not really."

And I believed him. In the months I'd worked for him, besides his lunch dates that turned out to not be dates at all, he had no social life that I'd seen. He was all work and no play. Emails in my inbox Monday morning were often dated over the weekend at all hours of the day and night.

"You should do something fun this weekend. There's so much to do here. You're really missing out."

"What do you have planned?" he asked.

I hadn't really made plans, but it seemed like the perfect time to come up with some. "It's supposed to be a sunny weekend, so I was thinking of going to the Space Needle. You can come with me."

He froze and turned to me. Our eyes locked, and immediately my skin began to pebble as goose bumps spread across my skin.

"Did you have to say it like that?" he said, but his voice was lower.

"What?" He quirked a brow at me and I thought back on my words, my face heating up when I realized. "You can come with me to the Space Needle, not come with me."

He reached out and ran his fingertips across my skin, making it flare up again. "I'd rather do the latter."

I swallowed hard, trying to push back the desire to lean into his chest, to press my lips to his. "I'm sure you would, but that's not the invitation that's on the table."

His eyes were hooded. "You need to be clearer before you speak, then. I was more than willing to help you come. With me. Many times."

I bit down on my lower lip, trying to ignore the ache between my legs. It was a talent I knew he was very capable of delivering on, and I did want it, very much so.

"The underground tours are awesome," I continued on in an attempt to change the topic, to turn down the blaze that was surrounding us.

"Underground what?" he asked.

"The city."

The crease in his brow deepened. "What?"

I sighed and rolled my eyes. "Do you know anything about Seattle after eight years?"

His lips formed a thin line, and he quirked a brow. "The weather."

"And?" I pressed.

"The view of the Sound at night."

"The Sound is beautiful at night."

Silence took over for a moment before he spoke again. "There is a fantastic view from my condo."

I froze for a moment, the butterflies kicking up in my stomach again. "That almost sounds like an invitation."

His gaze met mine. "It is. It includes food and as many orgasms as you can stand."

"A very nice invitation," I said, my voice just above a whisper.

"I'm a nice guy."

"When you want to be."

His lips twitched up into a smirk. "True." He leaned back and stared at me. "Is there something you want to tell me, Miss Prescot?"

I bit down on my lower lip in disbelief of what I was thinking of doing, of offering. "What if I wanted to see the view? Is there anything stopping that?"

He shifted his position and ran his fingers across his lips, drawing my gaze. I wanted both of them on me. "You. A professional relationship, remember?"

"I changed my mind."

"No, you haven't," he argued.

"No, I haven't, but what I said I wanted then was a lie. The truth never changed."

He was still as he regarded me, trying to figure out where I was going. "And what is that?"

I leaned in close, so close that his arm came around me, pulling me closer. "I can't stop thinking about you."

His lips crashed against mine, and his arms wrapped around my waist, pulling me until our chests met, mouths open, tongues lashing, and moans coming from both of us. Months of holding back exploded in a consuming passion I'd never experienced.

When he pulled back, we were both breathing hard.

"Tell me you want me," he said as his lips ghosted mine.

"I want you," I admitted.

"Lincoln."

"I want you, Lincoln."

The expression that flitted across his features was unrecognizable, but his lips, his body, told me everything.

Lincoln Devereux wanted me more than I ever imagined.

And for some reason, that scared me.

CHAPTER 15

Lincoln

I GOT SHAFTED, AND NOT IN A GOOD WAY.

Nothing happened after our make-out session on the deck of the yacht except blue balls that were making me an even crankier asshole.

Being on a boat in the middle of the water kept us from doing anything and by the time the boat returned, Ivy was falling asleep on her feet.

All I wanted to do was take her back to my place, but she was too tired.

Since then, she avoided me as best she could. Never getting too close, her eyes failing to meet mine. When they did, she crumbled under my gaze.

A week had passed and with each passing day she dodged me. By Thursday I was going out of my mind. My normally straight-talking, candid assistant was playing coy and seeming contrite.

I thought we had a moment. I thought we were moving

onto something more, but instead, she slammed the door in my face. Whatever happened was suddenly gone, almost as if she regretted letting her guard down. I was half expecting her to blame it on the champagne, but I knew that was the real Ivy with me.

The intern, whatever her name was, only seemed to create a barrier in the office.

"Miss Prescot!" I yelled out.

Agitation vibrated, pulsing with the blood in my veins, searching for any outlet.

"Yes, Mr. Devereux?"

"Where the fuck are the reports from accounting?"

"I'm sorry, sir. The phone has been ring—"

I cut her off, not wanting to hear. "I don't give a fuck about your excuses. Get me the reports, now."

She nodded before turning and racing out.

Fuck. Fuck. Fuck.

Things couldn't continue the way they were. I was pushing her further away, the opposite of what I needed.

I needed her closer, to get her to open up her legs—

Open up about Dante.

Fuck. Even my thoughts of revenge had turned into hunger for her pussy. I didn't want just knowledge about Dante. I wanted to know her.

"Where's my lunch?" I asked when she returned with a stack of files a few minutes later.

"It's eleven-thirty."

I narrowed my gaze on her. "Is that supposed to mean something?"

She backed up. "I'll go get it right now."

It was her fault. She drove me to the beastly attitude that

I was overcome with. It compounded with every day she kept her distance.

"Why do you keep coming in?" I spat an hour later when she crossed my threshold.

"Because you asked me to," she snapped back. It was the first sign of her feisty personality I'd seen all week. Maybe if I kept pressing it, she would push back.

"Go get my dry cleaning."

"I'll send Stacey," she said as she tapped on her phone.

"Who?" Who the fuck was Stacey?

"The intern."

I often forgot about the little mouse that occupied a desk outside my office. Every time I looked at the girl, I was tempted to yell "Boo" at her just to see what would happen.

"I didn't tell the intern to go, I told you."

"She can't direct your calls."

"Then have them go to voicemail for half a fucking hour. You can have her get me a coffee while you're gone."

"Yes, sir." Her tone was hard. I begged for her to hit back and maybe, just maybe, we could get back on track, because our working relationship had become a shit show.

A few minutes later the little mouse appeared, skittish as always in my presence. Why did I have an intern in the first place? Or was she Miss Prescot's? What was her purpose?

"Your coffee, sir," she said in that meek voice.

Fuck, did she remind me of someone. Someone I tried hard not to think about, but there she was, in a way, standing in front of me in the guise of the intern. Young, shy, unsure, and out of her element. Sweet and innocent and ripe for the picking from the less savory people of the world.

"Thank you," I said. The gesture seemed to make her

happy, and she smiled as I brought the cup up to my lips.

What filled my mouth could not be called good, let alone coffee.

I leaned over and grabbed my trash can, spitting the vile taste from my mouth.

"What the fuck is this?"

"Y-your coffee, sir?"

I narrowed my eyes at her. "This is swamp water filtered through a dirty sock. Do it again, and it better be right."

She backed up. "Yes, sir. Right away."

Fuck, just when I was thinking how vulnerable she was I lashed out, attacking her like the less savory people I envisioned.

Ivy walked in a few minutes later, coffee in hand. "You couldn't wait or just have her pick it up from downstairs, could you?"

"You are my assistant. I pay you to assist."

She folded her arms in front of her. "You don't pay me to be a punching bag."

"What is that supposed to mean?" I asked, loving the feel of the fire rolling off her.

"It means you have a stick up your ass this week, and I want to know why."

"You're out of line, Miss Prescot." She knew damn well what the issue was.

"And you're being an asshole, Mr. Devereux."

I ignored her comment, because it was the truth. "I'm trying to do my job. Go do yours."

For the remainder of the day I tried to avoid her at all costs, and she seemed to do the same. At six I called Austin to retrieve her and told her to go home, but it was nearly nine by the time I finally left the office.

The moment I was inside my home, I immediately changed and made my way down to the gym. I needed to let go on something.

The fitness center in my building was empty, and I was able to take over the speaker system. Music pumped hard, fast, and loud as I strapped on the gloves. I didn't bother warming up. I needed the release that only happened when my fist met BOB.

Sometimes it was nice that it had a face. Often, I imagined it was Dante's.

With each hit, the knot in my stomach loosened. By the time sweat dripped down my face, my frustration had turned from Ivy to Dante.

I was stunted in my search for dirt, for information that would crush him. I needed to find the key to destroying him.

I needed my revenge.

At that thought, every last ounce of strength was funneled into my fist for a final blow.

BOB took the hit, but there was so much strength in that last hit that the dummy tipped enough that gravity sent him down to the ground.

My chest expanded in large gasps as I bent over and stared at the weighted silicone at my feet.

"Evening, Lincoln."

I looked up to find Charlie, one of the few familiar neighbors I had. It was probably due to running into him occasionally in the gym.

"Evening." I straightened and tried to regain my breath.

"Women issues?"

I let out a chuckle. "How could you tell?"

"Because you almost killed BOB," he said before continuing. "It's not that you don't usually abuse him pretty bad, but this time he may need a hospital."

I shook my head and chuckled as I looked at the dummy lying on the ground. "He was looking at me funny."

"I bet. Want to talk about it?"

I shook my head. "Classic boy-likes-girl, but girl wants a professional relationship." Somehow, the light atmosphere had me opening up to him. I didn't really know him, but that seemed to help in the situation. He didn't know me, and he didn't know her, which gave him a different perspective.

"Yikes. She's not interested in you? Man, that sucks."

"I don't think it's that. There's interest and definitely a physical chemistry, but, well, I'm her boss. Her direct boss."

"Mixing business with pleasure. I see the dilemma now." He stepped on one of the treadmills and hit a few buttons. The belt whirred to life, and he began walking at a moderate pace.

"I almost had her convinced, but then the spell lifted and now it seems her default setting is avoidance. That just pisses me off even more, so I have resorted to a nasty attitude that is too much for her to handle, so she's calling me an asshole. I know she's partially right—hell, I am an asshole—but what's going on with her is different. I don't know if she realizes that or feels the same though." The words spilled out. It felt good to release them. I hadn't confided in anyone in years. Trust was hard-earned with me, and the only one who had mine on all levels, personal and professional, in Seattle was Koa.

"Ouch on the asshole part."

"It was far from the first time," I explained.

"You let her talk to you like that?"

"It's the truth." I let out a huff. "The messed-up part is that I don't want her—and I do want her."

"So, she's a conquest?"

"No, because I *do* want her. I very much want her. I don't *want* to want her, that's the problem, but she's that perfect trifecta." How did she have me so fucked up inside? The dichotomy of wanting her and not wanting her was exhausting. Mostly because all I wanted lately was her, but if I didn't have her it wasn't going to hurt her as much when everything collapsed.

"And what's your trifecta?" he asked as he increased the speed.

The three things that she bowled me over with the day of her interview. "Beauty, brains, and a backbone."

"She's your kryptonite, huh?"

"I guess you could say that."

"Kryptonite isn't always a bad thing. Sometimes it's the thing you need to survive."

I couldn't tell him that I was beginning to think my kryptonite was exactly that—necessary for my life. That thought filled my chest with dread because I knew I'd already started something that would turn her against me.

After a few more minutes of idle chat, I headed up for a shower. As the spray rained down on me, I thought back on what he said.

Charlie was right—Ivy was my kryptonite. She was a danger to me, to those feelings I didn't want to have, but some part of me wanted those feelings.

Some part of me was dying just to have her touch me.

I craved more than just a physical relationship, more than a work relationship. I wanted more. I wanted Ivy to be mine.

CHAPTER 16

Ivy

I MESSED UP. I SLIPPED, THEN I TRIPPED, AND THEN I JUST blew up my professional and personal relationship with Lincoln Devereux, all with one little confession. The disaster of my backpedaling was evident for an entire week in his mood.

After spending countless hours in the evenings talking with Iris, it was time to own up to the mess I'd made of my working relationship. Still, after all the conversations with my sister, after all the encouragement from Iris, taking our relationship to a personal level was a frightening thought.

As much of a pain as he could be, as much as I put him in his place, there was still doubt in my mind. What if our attraction wasn't really there? What if it was all a product of the one taste we had, but in the months that had passed, it was only the embers that remained? Even worse—what if it was only physical?

I knew the last one wasn't true. Over the months he'd

grown on me. Little things he did, said, that added up. Granted the bad mood version of him was greater, but I had a feeling that had more to do with the weight on his shoulders than me.

I couldn't let him stew for a second weekend, so on Friday I decided it was time to fix things.

"We need to talk," I said as I stepped in with his afternoon coffee.

He continued whatever he was doing, not even glancing at me. "That's an interesting choice of words in an interesting order."

"It's apt."

"There's *that* word again. I think that's in the top ten most used words of your vocabulary outside of the basic gender pronouns, numbers, and filler words."

I ground my teeth. "It's the most applicable word."

"That is also the most appropriate."

I crossed my arms in front of me. "Stop being a mocking ass."

"That is also apt," he said, still refusing to look at me.

"You're still in a mood."

"And I wonder why," he spat back.

"That's what I want to talk about."

There was a pause in his movements before he responded. "Going to renege?"

"I..." I trailed off. Things weren't going the way I wanted. The conversation had gotten askew, and he'd gotten to the bottom line before I had a chance to explain myself.

"If that's your answer, then get out. I have work to do."

"Lincoln, please."

There was a sudden smack as his hand slammed down on the desk. The action was aggressive and made me jump. I had never been physically intimidated by him, but something about his mood had me thinking it was definitely time to err on the side of caution. And maybe it was also time to own up to my part in all the tension between us. Own up to it to him specifically, because no amount of avoidance or talking out the drama with my sister was going to right the quickly sinking ship that was us.

When he finally looked at me, he was scowling, but there was more than anger there. His jaw was locked tight, brow furrowed, lips downturned, and his eyes were on fire. "Don't use my name unless you mean it, Miss Prescot."

He was hurt and angry and lashing out at me without giving me a chance to explain. But as I stood there, my chest broke open.

I thought I'd decided not to be scared, to not care about the whispers, the things said about me, and, most importantly, wrecking the working relationship we'd developed over months of hard work. My head and heart were at war, while my body was begging for the simplest of touch.

I didn't know what came over me, but I couldn't stand to see that look on his face anymore. He had the most beautiful smile, and it wasn't seen nearly enough.

Our eyes were locked, his watching me carefully as I leaned over and cupped his face. There was a spark that passed between us when our lips met. Soft, tender, but when he pressed forward to deepen the kiss, I released him, stepping back before he could grab hold of me, before that spark turned into an inferno.

"What the fuck was that?" he asked as he stared at me.

"You're my boss. I don't know how to do this."

Without warning, he stood and stalked toward me.

Reaching out, he seized my wrist and tugged. I slammed into his chest and let out a squeak of surprise as I looked into his hooded eyes. My whole body tingled from my scalp to my toes.

"You know how to do this," he said as he cupped my face with one hand, the other wrapping around me, holding me close. "Just like before. It's easy. Effortless, like breathing. Just let go."

Only nothing had ever scared me before the way Lincoln did. No one had ever affected me the way he did, and it was frightening.

I drew in a ragged breath when his lips met mine. There was no need for the spark, the fire already lit. His eyes were open, staring into mine as his tongue lavishly lapped against my own. Heat spread through me as I melted into his touch. I bowed into him as my body gave in to what I truly wanted. Slow, deep, passionate—it was the most sensual kiss of my life.

"Come over for dinner," he said when he pulled back.

I could feel the warmth in my cheeks, and all I wanted was to pull him back down. To remind me again just how natural we were together. "I don't know if that's a good idea."

"I do. We can order in, go over some contracts, because I never stop working, and see what happens."

"You know, Dante said almost the same thing to me many times."

"But you don't like him the way you like me."

I couldn't stop the smile that spread on my face. "Who said I like you?"

"Ivy." He blew out a breath, his jaw ticking. "You expect me to tell you everything, to be honest, but you haven't been with me by your own admission. Let's talk. Come over for dinner."

"Dinner at your house sounds dangerous." And it was. There would be no stopping us from succumbing. If he touched me, I wouldn't let him stop until we were both satiated.

He held up his hand. "I solemnly swear that I am up to— no, wait—I solemnly swear that I will not bend you over the couch the moment you walk in."

"Only the couch?" I asked as I tried *not* to think about him doing just that.

"Any surface." His smile faltered. "All joking and sexual innuendos aside, will you please have dinner with me?"

My gaze bounced between his eyes, searching for something to calm my nerves. He was earnest, almost desperate. "Yes, because you asked so nicely."

"Hmm, so all I need to do is add 'please' to anything and you'll do it. Interesting."

I shook my head. "That's not how it works."

"If you say so," he said with that sexy smirk as he stepped away. As he walked back around his desk, he glanced at me, that smile still intact, and winked.

My stomach gave a flip. I was doomed.

⤜∽

After going home and changing into something more casual, and going over my makeup and hair and changing my casual clothes half a dozen times, I headed back downtown. My nerves rattled, the butterflies swarmed in my stomach, and every other second I asked myself if it was a good idea to be going to my boss's house.

When I arrived at the Madison Tower, I had to enter a special code to enter the parking garage. There was a visitor section of the garage, and I parked before getting on the el-evator that led to the lobby, since I didn't hold a key to use the tenant elevator. Once inside, security had to validate me, which was a whole process of calling Lincoln and checking my ID before finally giving me a temporary card to get me up to the Penthouse floor.

When I arrived, there were only two doors, and standing at the open one was Lincoln. He'd changed into jeans and a T-shirt, his feet bare. There was something about the way he was standing, or maybe the casualness of his clothes, that turned up the heat inside me. The urge to jump into his arms and forget all about my fears was strong. How was I going to keep my hands to myself, let alone his?

For a fraction of a second, he didn't look like the imposing CEO of a large company, but an average guy.

"Hi," he said with a smile that made my knees go weak.

He held the door open, and I walked through while try-ing not to notice the electricity that buzzed as I passed him. "That's quite a few hoops to go through just to get up here."

"It won't be like that next time," he said as he closed the door and locked it. "I don't invite many people up here, so the security is strict. The last thing I want is an interloper."

I ignored the "next time" comment. "So, I'm special?"

"Yes."

I stopped in my tracks and found myself staring at the wall at his simple statement. My stomach dropped as I gazed upon all the photos decorating the space. There were a few on the shelves, but the walls were covered down the hall and in the living room.

In all of them was a blonde woman. Some contained him as well. They were smiling and happy in every single photo.

It was a hit to my system, a shot to my heart. It felt like the floor was falling out from beneath me as I scanned them. The photos weren't recent. He looked younger, and younger still in others. There was one with the two of them as teenagers, arms wrapped around each other in what looked like prom wear.

Who was she? More importantly, who was she to him?

He had continued walking, but halted when he noticed I was no longer behind him. "Ivy?"

"Who is she?" I asked, needing to stem the stream of questions that were running through my mind.

"No one."

There were dozens, not just a few. It was overkill for a "no one."

"Obviously she's someone to you."

The sheer amount spoke to that. Candid shots, goofy poses, and a clear connection.

"It doesn't matter. She's not here anymore." His voice was icy, his words cryptic, and they did nothing to stop the weight of the discovery from crushing me. Photos of a woman he was with from at least high school adorned his walls in a place he had lived for four years, and it didn't matter?

"Of course it matters." I set my purse on the floor and gestured to the photos. "Is that why not many people have been up here? Did you bring dates up here and they saw this wall?"

"I don't bring people up because they ask questions about things I don't want to talk about." He was coiled tight, but it wasn't just anger.

The storm waging behind his words kept me from pressing forward, from getting my answer. A part of me wasn't sure I wanted it, but I needed it if we were going to give in to these feelings. By the shrine he'd erected, it was obvious he was still hung up on whoever she was.

One thing I knew—I wasn't her.

"I was promised a view," I said, swallowing my curiosity, my need for answers. For the moment, at least.

The clash of wills lessened, and he relaxed, but I noticed the way his eyes flickered to the photos before he reached out for my hand. As I slipped my hand in his, a warm buzzing radiated from that point all the way up my arm, then cascaded down through my body.

I'd experienced the feeling before, but never on such a concentrated, consuming level. It was crippling to think that maybe he felt it too, but for her and not me.

I bottled it up and finally took a look around. His home was huge, and definitely qualified for the name of penthouse. My entire apartment could sit in his great room. Not that I minded. I loved my apartment.

Everything was lush and the decorations were minimal. It was clean and crisp like out of an HGTV show, with the exception of all the photos.

As we passed a fireplace in the center of the space and approached the glass walls, my mouth dropped open. The view was beyond spectacular, and we were still inside. He opened a door, and we stepped out onto a balcony that held a few couches and tables. The air still held some warmth to it as I stared out at the horizon.

The sun had just set, but the glow still reflected on the water, across buildings, and illuminated snowcapped mountains in the distance.

"So beautiful," I said as I stared at the perfect rainbow of colors in the sky.

"I told you it was good," he said as he leaned on the

banister and looked out.

We stood there, staring out, taking in the view until the last vestige of light in the sky was gone. I continued to look around at all the lights twinkling in the darkness, boats gliding into nothingness, and the Ferris wheel as it spun.

It struck me how nice it was to just be with him, without caution or worry. He stood next to me, but we didn't have to say or do anything. Even when I leaned into him for warmth, my head on his shoulder, he turned his head and pressed his lips to the top of my head.

Such a simple gesture that meant so much. It made my heart skip.

His stomach rumbled, startling us both, and we chuckled. "I guess that's our cue to look at menus. Can I get you a glass of wine?"

"That would be great."

I followed him into the kitchen, trying to avoid looking at the wall of questions and instead marveled at the chef's kitchen that could also possibly be the size of my apartment. Maybe that was an exaggeration, but not by much. The center island alone was larger than my bed.

Visions of laying back on it with Lincoln between my thighs flashed into my mind, and I had to chastise myself.

Talk first, then maybe other things. We weren't going any-where until I knew about the mysterious woman.

"Why do you have such a big place if it's just you?" I asked as I hopped onto one of the plush bar stools and let my elbows rest on the beautiful marble counter.

His brow furrowed as he pulled a bottle of wine from the fridge and set it down. "I'm not really sure. I guess I thought it was the thing to do at the time. There is way too much space, rooms I don't even go in. I definitely don't need 3,400 square feet to myself."

"Seems an awful lot of still, quiet space." Did he buy it for her?

"It's my sanctuary," he said as he stepped away to grab two glasses from the cabinet. "It's the one place I can be myself, the one place that knows me."

"I want to know you."

His lip quirked up as he pried the cork from the bottle. "How long do you think you'll be with me?"

"What do you mean?" I asked, more than a little confused by the sudden change of topic.

"You're a deadly combination of beauty and brains. I can't imagine you want to be my assistant forever."

"I love being an assistant."

He raised a brow at me as he began pouring the wine.

"Seriously," I added.

"You have leader potential."

I shook my head. "I don't want to be a leader. I like being the right-hand to the leader, as long as I get respect and recognition."

"But that won't always happen. You'll become resentful." He set a glass in front of me before pouring his own.

I shook my head as I swirled the wine around the glass. "Maybe I could run a company, but the biggest hurdle is that I don't want to. I'm not a leader, I'm an orchestrator. There's a difference. You're commanding and strong and have all the qualities to run a hundred-million-dollar company. I'd rather be by your side helping you make it happen."

"I like you beside me."

My eyes met his, and a familiar heat spread through my

body. "I like being beside you."

"Are you going to explain why you haven't been acting like it this week?" he asked, bringing up one of the reasons I agreed to cross his threshold.

I blew out a breath before taking a sip, letting the myriad of flavors play on my taste buds. "Have you ever wanted something, but you were scared it would ruin something else when you finally got it?"

He nodded. "Every single time I think about you."

His admission caught me off guard. "How much do you think about me?"

His gaze bored into mine. "Much more than I should."

"Should?"

He let out a little chuckle before sitting on the stool next to me. "You are always so clever at picking up on things."

"A talent, I suppose," I said as I turned toward him.

"I finally understand. That's how you steered clear of Dante."

I nodded. "I could see his bullshit from a mile away."

"But you don't see mine," he said, his tone suddenly heavy again.

"What do you mean?"

His fingers ran down my arm, his eyes intently watching the goose bumps that appeared on my skin. "I meant it every time I called you a distraction. You have a power over me."

Our lips were inches apart, and I wanted to feel his against mine again. I filled the distance, leaning toward him. His mouth tasted like the wine, and each brush of his tongue against mine sent sparks straight down between my thighs.

As I leaned back, light glinted off something, catching my eye. I turned to look, only to find the photos of him with the other woman staring back at me. There were so many.

She was special.

I couldn't see *his* bullshit, yet it was staring at me from across the room. I was just a distraction. That was all.

I pushed back and stepped away before he could pull me in again.

"Ivy?" his brow scrunched.

The weight of the eyes, of the rock sitting on my chest. I couldn't stay. "Who is she?" He had to tell me, or there was no stopping me.

He shook his head. "No."

"Earlier you were talking about honesty and now you won't even tell me the name of a woman whose face is plastered all over your home!" I threw my arms up and waited. "Do you love her?"

He didn't need to answer me. I could see it in his eyes. The blatant refusal to tell me one thing, closing the door on the conversation, left me no other choice.

Like Austin once said, he had secrets, and I wasn't about to be one, to be the other woman. That was the only way left to feel, because even if he wasn't with her, she was all he could think about. If I couldn't stop thinking about the woman in the photos, then it was obvious that neither could he.

"I…I have to go."

I moved to walk around him, but he reached out and grabbed my hand, halting me. "Ivy, wait."

"It's too much," I said, trying to keep the tears at bay.

"No, it's not."

"Yes, it is. I'm sorry, Mr. Devereux, but this is as far as we go." I pulled my hand from his and ran to the front door, picking up my purse from the floor as I went.

He called after me, followed me, but I ignored him. I ignored the ache in my chest.

Ignored the cracking of my heart.

I wasn't special.

I was stupid.

CHAPTER 17

Lincoln

FOR HOURS AFTER IVY LEFT, I WAS UNABLE TO DO ANYTHING other than stare at the door. I ran after her. Even after the elevator doors closed, and I raced down all twenty-four flights of stairs fucking barefoot.

Her taillights were all I saw as she exited the garage.

I couldn't sleep, my body and mind too wired, and everything was focused on one person. Her touch called me, her body. To be wrapped up in her was my dying man's wish.

More than to see Dante fall, I was accepting that I wanted Ivy as my own, but at what cost? Could I tell her about the photos that seemed to spark her escape?

Could I open up to her about London?

Hours passed, and I was even more worked up. My need for her had reached a level of desperation that I'd never experienced before. Even if it meant telling her, I would. Enough of the bullshit of the past few days. She told me she wanted me and then tried to take it back.

She agreed to come over, she kissed me, and she suddenly ran away.

Fuck that.

I was angry when I dialed her number, barely realizing what I was doing.

"'Ello?" she said in a sleepy voice.

"Where are you?" I asked.

Another sleepy noise. "Mr. Devereux?"

"Answer me."

"At home. In bed. Asleep."

"I'm coming over." I walked down the hall to my bedroom to grab some shoes.

"Okay…wait, what?" she asked, finally more awake. "It's two in the morning."

"I'll be there in ten minutes."

"The hell you will. Go to sleep, Mr. Devereux."

The line went dead, but it didn't matter—I already had my keys in hand and was out the door.

My skin crawled. The itch, the need to have her beneath me, was intolerable. Nothing but satiating the bone-deep desire for her would help, and there were no substitutions.

I was going to fuck her tonight. I needed to.

Thankfully I had her address in my contacts, and I pulled up the map. She was surprisingly close in Pioneer Square, and it only took a few minutes to arrive. There was a parking lot behind her building, and I found her car before taking the spot next to it. An exterior staircase led to the second story, and an interior hall leading to the apartment doors.

Her apartment was on the end, close to one of the staircases. I slammed my fist against the door, the sound ringing out down the corridor. I didn't care if it woke everyone in the building up, they could all fuck off, but I needed her.

Suddenly the large metal door flew open, and there she was. Her hair was disheveled, and she was wearing only a tiny pair of shorts and a tank top.

"What?" she cried out before grabbing my shirt and pulling me inside. She slammed the door shut before turning and glaring at me. "Are you trying to get my neighbors pissed at me?"

I didn't respond. There was one reason I was there, and one alone.

"You promised," she cried out as my hand slipped beneath the fabric of her skimpy tank top.

Her skin was warm, her breasts soft as I cupped one, reveling in the feel of her nipples tightening as my fingers swiped across them.

"You've been playing me for days," I hissed into her ear as I nipped the flesh below. "You told me you wanted me, too." I gripped her breast hard before dragging my hand down her stomach and around her hip to do the same to her ass.

"You're keeping things from me. I won't play that game," she said before drawing in a sharp breath when my other hand slipped between her legs.

A growl left me as I pressed my fingers against her clit, then slapped it.

"This is not a game."

"Then what is it?"

"Want. Need. Desire. The unimaginable urgency to be buried deep in this perfect pussy."

"How do you know that's what I want?" she asked.

I slipped my hand beneath the fabric of her shorts and found her slick and swollen. "Because I'm the only one who can make you this wet."

"Fuck you."

Her resistance only made me want to manhandle her, to throw her against the wall and beat my cock into her. "Every day. Multiple times a day. Everywhere."

"Stop."

My eyes closed at the word, and despite the vibration in my veins, I stopped moving. It would tear me apart, but if that was what she wanted, I would do it.

"Do you really want me to?"

"Y-yes."

My eyes screwed tight and I pulled my hand from her, internally cursing everything.

Her hands cupped my face, and she smashed her lips to mine.

The shock had my eyes open and I pulled back, needing clarification because her actions were wildly different. "Yes, what?"

"Every day. Everywhere," she said on a breath.

"Thank fuck."

I crashed back into her lips before spinning her and bending her over while pinning her hands to the wall with one of my own. I freed my cock and I pulled a condom from my pocket and tore it open with my teeth.

"Tell me again how you want this, want me inside you," I said as I tugged her shorts down and pressed the head of my dick against her slit, coating it with her juices.

"Fucking fill me," she said and I could swear it was a growl.

Using my free hand, I lined up and wasted no time slamming in. Her cry was a shot of heat that made my toes curl.

I pulled out and sat at the edge of her opening. "Say my name."

"Lincoln," she said on a breathy moan.

A wave of warmth spread through my chest, and I slammed back in.

"Again."

"Lincoln."

Fucking perfection.

Every thrust drove me, every one of her high-pitched squeals spurred me to drill her harder and deeper.

Fuck. It was exactly the release I needed.

I let go of her arms, gliding my hand down until I cupped her neck and pulled her head toward me, forcing her back to arch even more. I loved the way her pussy tightened around me with even the slightest cupping of her neck. Even her nipples hardened. One breast fit my hand perfectly, the nipple slipping between two fingers and allowing me to pinch making her let out a high, sweet moan.

It was the sound of an angel.

The sight of her ass bouncing with each slam of my hips against her was hypnotic.

I tugged on her hair, forcing her head back.

"Tell me you love it," I hissed as I slammed into her.

"I love it."

"What do you love?"

"Mmm... Fuck. Your cock. I love your cock."

With a scream, her body tensed and shuddered as her orgasm rocked through her.

Seconds later, her knees gave out and I wrapped my arms around her while I walked us to the bed. She collapsed down to the mattress, unable to hold herself up, but I couldn't stop, driven by the need to fill her, and continued to drill into her until I tensed, pleasure wracking me as I fired off.

I was completely drained and fell beside her on the bed.

The second time with her was even more fantastic than the first. I didn't want to stop, but not stopping meant I had to truly open up to her.

Could I really do it? Could I give myself into these feelings? Did anything good ever come from loving someone? I watched them destroy my everything in the blink of an eye.

The image of the last time I saw her was forever etched in my mind.

I will never be whole again.

"Come on, let's shower," Ivy said once we'd calmed down before turning from me and slipping off the bed.

I reached out for her and grabbed her hand. It was instinctual. A need to calm whatever knot had settled in my chest.

"I'm sorry," I blurted out, not sure why, but with the air I felt rolling from her, it felt necessary.

She turned to me, her pale skin still flushed and a spark of anger in her eyes.

"For what? Waking me at two in the fucking morning so you could get off, or for being a complete fucking ass to me all week?"

My hand tightened around hers. "Both."

"I walked out for a reason. If you want to stay, then explain yourself, because I will not tolerate this shit, and while you're at it, tell me who she is."

My brow scrunched as I stared at her. "Who?" I tried to play it off, but it was pointless. She'd only stormed out of my home hours before.

"Stop playing stupid. You know who. The woman in the

photos all over your house. The one you refuse to tell me about. Is she your wife? Girlfriend?"

I shook my head. "I don't have those, you know that."

"Then who is she to you? Because I can't do this if she's someone special."

"She is special."

Ivy blew out a breath and turned from me, her arm pulling, attempting to release her hand from my grip.

"Get out."

"Ivy—"

"Get out!" She wrenched her hand from mine and crossed her arms over her chest. "You said you weren't going to do that, and I *won't* take it anymore, so leave."

"Do what?"

"Shut down on me. That was why I left."

"I'm not shutting down, but there are also things I don't talk about. I don't invite many people into my home because, as I'm sure you've noticed, I don't have anyone I'd really call a friend. I'm just a lonely asshole sitting on the highest peak looking down at the world."

She threw her hands up as she shook her head, her teeth mashed together. "I can't do this, Lincoln. I don't think I can work for you anymore."

My heart slammed in my chest. I had to tell her, tell her more than I wanted to, if I wanted to keep her.

Keep her?

I'd thought them, the words. I gave a voice to them, and admitted to myself that Ivy wasn't just some tool. More than wanting to keep her as my assistant, I wanted to keep her beside me and in my bed.

"Wait, please…just wait." I bent over the edge and dug

my wallet from my jeans. Opening it up, I found the photo of London I kept with me and held it out.

"Her?"

Ivy nodded.

I stared down at the photo and let the pain wash over me. It was my fuel, what drove me to succeed.

"She is very special to me. She's the reason behind everything, how my life has been shaped."

Ivy huffed. "Lincoln, I don't—"

"Let me explain," I growled, cutting her off.

She blinked at me and nodded. "Who is she?" she asked again.

The only way out of the mess of doubt in me I'd created was to tell her my most agonizing secret.

"My twin sister."

A gasp filled the air, and, in my periphery, I watched her drop down next to me. I couldn't look at her, couldn't take the pity I knew would be in her eyes after my next words.

"And she's dead."

Ivy had an identical twin sister, and therefore was one of the few people who would understand why her death wrenched me so badly. Of all the people I knew, Ivy was one of the few who would understand the lifeline that was frayed and torn that no longer connected me to someone else.

Ivy reached out and placed her hand on my forearm. "What happened?"

"Eight years ago, she killed herself." My breathing became labored as it did every time I talked about her. "I knew something wasn't right. I could feel it, like a weight on my chest. We had that connection." I looked to her and she nodded. "For months I had felt down, depressed. It started before then, but it was so bad those last few months I considered going on an antidepressant. I would have dreams of being buried alive and wake up struggling to breathe."

"How awful."

I nodded. "I was in a meeting with a client when my phone rang. I had to silence it, but as soon as the meeting was over, I checked to see who it was. As soon as I saw her name, the odd feeling in my chest opened up into a chasm. She wasn't answering, wouldn't respond to texts. I left work and took the first flight out here. During the flight, that hole got deeper and darker and colder. I managed to convince the super at her building to let me in."

My breath stuttered. In eight years, I hadn't told a soul.

"Lincoln, stop," Ivy said in a soft voice, her fingers making soothing circles on my skin.

I looked into her eyes. I'd gone that far. I needed to finish, to get all that I could divulge out.

"I'll never get that scene out of my mind." Images flashed behind my eyes, and I had to squeeze them tight. A sea of red, London's hazel eyes staring blankly. Jumping into the water and screaming at her, begging her not to leave me. "She slit her wrists in the bathtub."

Ivy let out a gasp.

"I couldn't save her. If only I had picked up her call. If only I had gotten her to open up. I knew something was wrong, but she kept telling me everything was fine."

"It's not your fault."

"Why would she do that?" The pain had taken over. Telling Ivy was as cathartic as it was torturously painful. "We were each other's everything. People don't understand, they don't get it, but of all the people I know, you're the only one who can truly understand. London wasn't just my sister, she was my other half. From the beginning, it was me and her. Now it's just me. I still have Dakota, but she…"

"She can never be to you what London was."

I shook my head. "I love Dakota, but we were never close like me and London. I play the role of big brother with her, not closest confidant."

Ivy made soothing strokes on my arm. "They say that the death of a twin is akin to the death of a spouse. Not the same, but the depth of connection and grief are similar. Being a twin is a powerful emotion. I'm lonely without Iris, but I also know she's only a phone call or text away. I can only assume that your loneliness is a hundredfold times that."

"It's only superseded by the anger."

"At her?"

I shook my head and sighed. "I have her picture everywhere to remind myself why I work so hard. Why every day I strive to make DCS a giant."

"But her photo isn't in your office."

"There are pictures of her there, but for reasons I'm not ready to disclose, I keep them hidden."

The curiosity sat in her eyes, but she nodded in acceptance. "She was beautiful."

"She was my sunshine." *My only sunshine*, I thought, the tune playing out in my head. "She'd battled depression in college, and because of that, so did I. People thought it was the other way around. Nobody believed she suffered from it because she was always just this ray of light."

That he snuffed out.

Ivy climbed onto my lap and spread my arms and as my muscles resisted, I noticed just how wound up I'd become. Her hands moved up my arms, across my shoulders, up my neck until she was cupping my face.

"Shh, calm," she whispered.

It was a tactic she used at the office. Like a drug, a tranquilizer, I was immediately calmed.

"How do you do that?" I asked as I wrapped my arms around her and rested my forehead on hers.

"At first, it was an experiment, and the absolute confusion on your face was priceless, but it calmed you. After a few times with the same result I began to wonder if you were deprived."

"Deprived of what?"

"Human connection," she said. She was so unbelievably right. "You work so hard, so long, every day. As far as I can tell, you spend your free time working or working out, and that's it."

"Before you, there were women."

She gave a small nod. "I know."

"No matter what, they only took the edge off. They couldn't do what you do."

"What do I do?"

I ghosted my lips against her. "Make me feel again. More than the anger and pain that's consumed me for years. It disarms me."

"I want to take it all away."

My fingers spread out on her back, and I pulled her as close to me as I could. "You can't. It will consume you as well."

"Then I want to help carry it."

"Don't say that."

"Why not?"

"Because I'm only going to hurt you." For the briefest of moments, I'd forgotten what I'd put into motion. What was happening elsewhere as we sat there.

"No, you won't," she argued. Her beautiful eyes were practically begging me.

I brushed her hair back and cupped her face. "Yes, I will. You'll hate me and these feelings will turn to ash."

"What feelings?"

I shook my head. "If I speak them, you will want to convince me that this can work."

"We could work."

"We could, but we can't." The more I was with her, the more I fell for her—my perfect storm.

She shook her head. "You're speaking in riddles, Lincoln."

I let out a groan. "Have I ever told you how much I love that?"

"What?"

"You saying my name."

"Lincoln," she said again.

I let out a groan as I buried my head into her neck and got lost in the feel of her arms wrapped around me.

It was the most comfort I'd found in almost a decade, and I sucked the feeling in like the starving man I was.

If only I could keep her for always.

CHAPTER 18

Ivy

T HE NEXT MORNING, I AWOKE TO ARMS WRAPPED AROUND me and the soft tickle of breath against my neck.

I knew the warmth that surrounded me. It was so familiar, so inviting from the first time I felt it. Having it in my bed, surrounding me, was more than perfection.

It was right.

I was afraid. Plagued by negative thoughts that pushed him away. I'd been so swept away by our moment on the yacht, but I doubted myself later, then him.

I'd led him on, and instead of retracting my admission, I played coy. Then I pulled back when I doubted his feelings after seeing the wall of what I had found out was his sister. It was no wonder he came apart at the seams.

Not that I didn't enjoy it, because he was a man possessed. Passion was a pale word to describe it. Earth-shattering, soul-unraveling joining. Pleasure that ripped everything apart only to stitch us back together.

But it wasn't as just Ivy and Lincoln, it was as something new. Something exciting and wonderful and full of hope.

The tickle of breath morphed into soft lips against my shoulder. Tender touches with a lingering burn.

"Good morning," he said, his voice rough from sleep.

"Mmm."

"Does coffee deliver here?"

My lips pulled up into a smile, and I shook my head. "Keurig."

"What's that?"

"Not an espresso machine, but takes the edge off."

His hand trailed down my side before slipping over the edge of my hip to the space between my thighs. I drew in a breath as his fingers swept across my clit.

"I know something else that can take the edge off," he whispered against my ear as he flexed his hips, pressing his hard length against me.

A moan slipped past my lips as I arched against him. His touch was fervent and assertive as it moved around my skin.

"Fucking beautiful," he whispered against my skin. His fingers slipped inside me, and I drew in a breath. "That's it. I want you close before I'm inside."

The assault of his fingers inside me, palm pressing against my clit, his mouth on my skin, and his fingers pinching my nipples had me there, on edge, in no time at all.

I let out a whimper when he pulled his fingers from inside me, but it turned into a groan as he pushed into me, stretching me, filling all of me. My head fell back against his shoulder as he pulled out, then slammed back in.

I felt so full of him, and it was perfection.

The hand that had been on my breast trailed up to cup

around my neck. He gave a light squeeze that had me clamping down around him. Little nips from his teeth moved up my neck until his breath was hot against my ear.

"You're mine. This pussy I'm fucking," his hand left my hip and lightly slapped against my clit, making me gasp, "is mine. All of it. All of you."

"Yes." Everything was fuzzy as he played my body, my muscles tensing as I grew closer.

"Tell me," he said as he nipped my jaw.

"I'm yours. I'm all yours, Lincoln."

"So fucking wet for me," he growled as he bit down on my shoulder, much harder than before.

A spark shot from that spot straight to my pussy. That was the final push and I was gone, shaking in his arms as he continued thrusting. His moans in my ear grew louder, his movements faster until I was suddenly empty.

Warm splashes landed on the back of my thighs, my ass, and even the entrance of my pussy.

He was breathing hard as he settled, his arms becoming heavy.

"I think it's time for that shower now," I said, earning a chuckle from the mercurial man behind me.

∞

A shower and an hour later, we were presentable and headed out for "acceptable" coffee and some breakfast.

There was a Lexus sitting next to my Chevy Cruze when we made it down the stairs, which confused me.

"Is that how you got here?"

The Lexus beeped, and he motioned for me to get in.

"How else would I get here?"

I shrugged. "I don't know. Austin? Weird, I know, but I didn't know you had another car besides the Continental."

"I own the Continental, but it is Austin's. This is my car."

Much like his apartment, the car was in immaculate condition. It looked like it barely had any wear, and I doubt it saw the road much.

What I thought might be a quick drive over to one of the local cafes turned into a trip on the I-5 and ending at a diner called Glo's.

We got out and I grabbed onto his outstretched hand, loving the warmth that passed. I was absolutely loving the casual ease that surrounded us.

"Quite a ways just for breakfast," I said, finally voicing my confusion of location choice.

"They have the best food. London and I discovered it by accident after a night of drinking when we were in college. Taxi driver knew just the place, and he was right."

A waitress seated us and I took a menu from her, scanning over all the delicious-looking food when it hit me.

"Wait, college?"

He nodded. "I graduated from the University of Washington."

I stared at him. How had I not known where he graduated from? All the homework I did on DCS and I never did look at his background.

"So you've lived here before."

Again, he nodded.

"And even then, you never went to the Space Needle?" I asked.

That made him laugh while I was still baffled that not only

had he lived in Seattle for eight years, he also apparently lived here at least another four years before that. It blew my mind.

"We didn't cross the water very often, stayed in the university area."

"Not even when you came out to visit the campus with your parents?" Who in the world lived in Seattle for a total of at least twelve years and never went to the observation deck of the Space Needle?

"Why is this so important to you?" he asked as he shook his head.

"I'm just surprised, is all, and wondering if you've ever really lived."

The waitress came over, and we ordered our lifeblood—coffee.

"How about you take me?" His fingers twined with mine on the tabletop, and I stared down at them, then to his eyes. The atmosphere was so relaxed, so different from before. I liked it, but all of the conversations from the day before swirled in my brain, confusing me as to what our status was after everything that was said.

"So, what is this?" I asked as I waved my hand between the two of us.

He looked up from the menu. "Breakfast."

"That's not what I'm asking, and you know it."

He pulled my hand to his lips. "I thought I was pretty clear this morning."

My heart did a double tap in my chest, and I squirmed a little in my chair as I remembered. He called me his, and every part of me knew it as truth.

"But you have a tendency to put a wall up, so what do you think this is?" he asked.

I pulled my bottom lip between my teeth. "I was confused the last week."

"Is that an 'I'm sorry, Lincoln.'"

"Only if I get an apology for your shitty attitude."

"It was your fault," he said with a smirk.

"Do you feel better?"

"Loads lighter." He winked at me.

My face heated, and I had to look away. "Then I'm sorry for how I've acted since the yacht."

"Ditto."

"But I'm not sorry for keeping it professional the last few months."

"It has been difficult not being able to touch you." Again, he intertwined our fingers, and the rightness of it blanketed me again.

Since the moment I bumped into him in the lobby, we had been working our way to that moment. The moment when I realized how much I wanted to be in his life out of the office as much as I was in, only in a different way. I wanted to be his, and I was.

We ordered breakfast and chatted about our established date to the Space Needle. We didn't talk about work or the office or how we were going to handle things come Monday morning.

Instead, we were just Ivy and Lincoln, talking about everything and nothing at the same time.

"You were a software developer with DCS before you became CEO, right?" I asked as I shook some salt onto my veggie and meat filled omelet, followed by some pepper.

He nodded as he cut into his Eggs Blackstone. "Most of our current systems come from software I created. They've changed and evolved over the years, but the original was mine."

"Wow, I didn't know that. When I worked for Dante, in the beginning, I used to think he was some brilliant developer. I mean, that was how he made his fortune, generated money to start Kilgore Industries."

At the mention of Dante, Lincoln tensed. "What changed your mind?"

You.

Lincoln didn't arrogantly shout from the rooftops his genius, unlike Dante, who was mostly talk.

"It was small things at first. He always gloated about this site he developed. Then one night, after a few drinks, he kept saying 'We were going to be as big as Facebook.' We. Not I— we. And if you were going to be that big, why would you sell out to them?"

"People will do anything for money."

"You think so?"

He nodded as he stabbed at his hash browns a little more forcibly than necessary. "It corrupts some, to the point they will betray friends and family. They will take lives for it and show no remorse."

I took his hand, stopping him before he broke the plate. "Sounds like you have some experience." I didn't know what Dante had done, why the rift between them, but there was some obvious bad blood.

He blew out a breath, finally relaxing back, and I returned to my breakfast. "Experience isn't always a good thing, though it has been my driving force."

"Well, I think you may be right," I said, deciding to reveal some of the things I'd learned before I left.

"Why is that?"

I took a sip of my coffee as I decided how to word it. "For five years, I watched him oversee the company developers, sell software that had constant issues, and many failed promises. He has a great mind for ideas, but not execution. Add in his penchant for getting what he wants, and the company is on shaky ground."

"Shaky ground?" That made him perk up. "I thought Kilgore was doing well."

"The financial reports said so, but they were wrong. He's squandered so much money on inconsequential things, on clients. He really has no head for business."

"Are you saying he's inflated his numbers?" he asked, much more interested than I expected.

"Oh, I don't know about that... Maybe, though. It all just makes me see the staggering difference between the two, and I'm proud to say I work for such an upstanding company."

"Glad to hear that, because I think I can say this with some sense of certainty that the CEO thinks highly of you."

"Does he, now?" I asked, playing along.

He nodded. "Very highly."

"Well, I think very highly of him as well."

He pressed his lips against my fingers again. "Good."

I learned several things about Lincoln over the next several hours, including the affectionate side of the executive.

By the time he headed home, he'd given me six more orgasms, and though I still wasn't sure of our relationship status, I had a feeling we would work it out later. After all, he had the stamina of a man half his age and was always looking for any and all ways to get inside me.

CHAPTER 19

Lincoln

T HE PLAN WOULD WORK. IT HAD TO.

As I sat in the restaurant a week later across from Marcus, the lawyer from the prosecutor's office who was spearheading the investigation based on information I provided, I began to doubt.

I thought having Ivy working for me would open up avenues to take Dante down, but the opposite happened. Something with a potentially far worse outcome.

While she was providing me with avenues for Marcus to look into, I had lost my target. My focus had shifted, morphed into longing and need for the flesh of a woman instead of the blood of my enemy.

"Why are we meeting in person? I thought that was too dangerous."

"We need to talk," Marcus said from the other side of the booth.

"Then talk."

"I don't know what has happened to you, but I need you to get your focus back."

"I don't know what you're talking about," I said as I straightened up.

He took a long pull from his e-cigarette, then blew out. "Like hell you don't. That new skirt is distracting you."

"She's our key," I argued as I slammed back the rest of my whiskey.

His dark eyes were narrowed in on me. "That may be, but, as I pointed out, she is a distraction."

"She isn't."

"Have you fucked her?"

I signaled to the waiter for another glass. "That's irrelevant."

"It's completely relevant. She's involved, even if she doesn't know it."

I shook my head and tapped my finger on the table. "You said get the information any way I could."

"I may have, but I didn't expect you to fall for her."

"I don't have feelings for her," I lied.

"Good. Then when she finds out you lied to her, broke her trust, and toss her aside as you claim no involvement, you won't have any regrets."

Fuck. I didn't like the way this conversation was going. I hated even more that he was reminding me the feelings I really did have were going to hurt her. Still, I didn't want to stay away. I couldn't bring myself to.

There was a heaviness filling my chest, and as much as I wanted to tamp it down, I couldn't, because it concerned Ivy. The feelings I'd developed for her were unexpected. She truly was my perfect woman.

Ivy was created out of clay and brought to life by Zeus

solely for me.

"You make me sound like a cold-hearted asshole."

"Lincoln, I've known you for six years, and the entire time you've had one focus—destroy Dante. It's one of the things I've admired about you. Doing anything and everything to reach your goal."

"And I am," I tried to reassure him. The problem was the guilt that sat on my chest.

"We will see."

"Enough. Why did you want to meet?"

Marcus adjusted his position and leaned in. "What little intel you've gleaned off your little strumpet has yielded some results. We've begun to investigate his finances."

"And?"

"And I'm beginning to wonder many things, the first being how they are reporting a profit."

If Kilgore was in such a bad position that they were falsifying their financial reports, that would be a strong nail in Dante's coffin, it would trickle down to anyone who touched those records.

Including past employees.

"I don't want any of this coming back on Ivy."

"Excuse me?" he balked at me.

"She has nothing to do with anything he has done." She had no idea. She had thoughts that something wasn't right, but that was all.

"I don't agree. She was his personal assistant for a good portion of the company's lifetime. Not to mention how suspicious it looks that she suddenly went to work for you."

"She has done nothing wrong," I stressed. I refused to let her take any blame for my actions.

"Then I suggest you get rid of her the moment things blow up. Otherwise, DCS could be investigated."

"They would find nothing."

"I agree, but it still wouldn't look good, and continuing to employ her draws attention. The best thing is to get rid of her as soon as things blow up. The further she is away, the less interested they'll be in her."

I hated that he was right.

"He's called her, multiple times."

"Jesus Christ, Lincoln." He sat back and circled his head around before blowing out a breath. "How?"

"Through the office."

"Whoever he gets as his defense lawyer will have a fucking field day if Dante decides to lay anything on her."

"I told you, there was no NDA. Any knowledge she decides to tell anyone, she is allowed to. It's Dante's fault for not protecting his ass." And if he even tried, I would be standing there in the way. He wasn't going to touch her, physically, emotionally, or legally.

"Do you just have her word on that?" he asked and I could almost see the questions swirling in his head.

"What do you mean?"

He held up his hand as a gesture to calm me, but it only put me more on edge.

"I'm playing devil's advocate here. I'm thinking like his lawyers and how far Dante would go. Forging her signature isn't beyond the pale. When things go down, you have to stay away. Can you do that?"

"Why wouldn't I?" I asked while I asked myself if I really could. Was it possible to push her away when the time came? To hurt her in order to keep her safe.

That was the key. I would do anything to keep her away from Dante's wrath.

"Because I see the look in your eye. Because you're pushing back, resisting, defending. Lie to me all you want, but you've told me today without saying it—she's more than just a tool. Whatever she is to you, however deep your feelings run, I'm sorry. Everything you worked for is in motion. There's no stopping this train. What happens to her, I don't know. Hopefully nothing, but a lot of that has to do with you. So, if you want to protect her, you have to stay away from her."

I said nothing, the weight of my actions holding me down. Ivy was so much more to me than I ever anticipated or dreamed she would be.

But would she understand? Would she forgive me for what was about to happen?

CHAPTER 20

Ivy

FINALLY KNEW. THE SECRET THAT HELD LINCOLN CAPTIVE. That whole night before he came over, I'd agonized over the woman in the photo. Looking at them again, there was something I hadn't picked up on. My own fears refused to let me see anything other than Lincoln with a beautiful woman plastered all over the place.

Not one photo showed them kissing, or her on his lap, or anything that would indicate something romantic. I had to chastise myself on that one, on blowing things up, but he'd been evasive and I hadn't understood why.

Their eyes were the same color, but I'd only picked up on the blonde of her hair.

The pain bled from him in words. They were carefully measured, but there was no hiding the absolute devastation her death created in him.

For the first time in months, I was finally getting an inside view of Lincoln Devereux. With his admission, I knew I was one of a select few, and that made me feel special.

The pain he endured on a daily basis I could only imagine as Iris's distance was an extremely pale comparison. But I knew the connection, the depth of having your life tied with another's. Twins and other multiples, no matter what kind, shared something no other siblings can understand. Even two-thousand miles away, I could still feel Iris, in a way.

I also finally understood him giving so much money to The London Foundation. He finally admitted to being the founder of the charity, in order to help those like him. When I researched him in the beginning I'd only glanced at what the foundation was about. It made mention of a woman named London, but no last name was given, no photo of her posted.

Since finding out who she was, his actions made more sense. There was an invisible cord, torn and frayed, hanging from Lincoln. Lifeless. He was hurt and had never processed his pain, never dealt with it. He channeled it all into his work.

Even more I wanted to help DCS. Lincoln had shown me just how good and special and honorable of a man he was. My moral standing with Kilgore was out the window for a much better cause and I was going to share everything I knew to help Lincoln grow DCS even bigger.

Complete and total domination of the market.

"Good morning, Miss Prescot," Lincoln said as he wrapped his arms around my waist, his lips pressing against my neck.

"Mr. Devereux, that is highly inappropriate," I teased as my neck listed to one side to give him more access.

He reached down, his hand slipping under my skirt until he was between my thighs. "I think we're getting there."

I turned in his arms, his hand moving with me while his other one grabbed my ass. "You better not get carried away.

Stacey will be here any minute."

"Who?" he asked as he pressed his fingers against my clit making me gasp.

"The intern." I rolled my eyes. He continued to move his fingers in slow, deliberate circles.

"Right. By the way, do you know why there is an intern in my office?"

A sigh left me. "Of all people, I thought you would know, but since you can't even be bothered to remember her name, I'm not surprised. She's in school for business administration. Technically, she's my intern."

"Can I see you tonight?" he asked, changing the subject, his eyes focused on my lips.

Since we erased the line, personal was bleeding into professional. Though I loved his touch, the office wasn't the most appropriate place. "'See, this is the trouble that gets started."

"What trouble?"

"What are you thinking about right now?"

He leaned down close to my ear, his fingers slipping under the thin fabric of my panties before sliding through my slick folds. "You hiding under my desk sucking the life from my cock. Eating you out as you're spread out on my desk. *Fucking* you on my desk."

I couldn't stop my hips from riding his fingers. "So, you're thinking about your desk."

"Technically, you and my desk," he said as his lips pressed against my neck again.

He was breaking me down. I was about ready to bend myself over my desk to get some relief. "Maybe I should leave you and your desk alone. It seems like you need it."

A growl left him as he pulled me closer, his fingers driving in deeper. "What I need, Ivy, is to be buried inside you all day, every day."

"But we'll never get any work done," I argued. My mind was so foggy, focused on the pleasure he provided.

"Maybe not, but it's infinitely more fun."

"True. Tell you what." I reached over, a moan crawling out when his fingers hit the perfect spot, and grabbed his coffee. "Take this, go to your office, and we'll talk about your little fantasies later." I held the cup out to him.

I could almost see the internal war waging within him. Me versus coffee. Sex versus caffeine. I pressed the edge of the cup to his lips and tipped it slightly back, making certain coffee won out.

It worked, a moan leaving him not because of sexual arousal, but because of the lifeblood known as the coffee bean as it took its hold. His fingers slipped from me and he stepped away, completely entranced by the magical brew.

Once he was away from me, I was able to calm down. Getting him away from me was difficult, because my body was begging for it, for him, but it wasn't the right time or place. I had to make sure to keep my distance from him, never let him get too close while at work. Otherwise, our attraction would take hold, and with no more barriers, all bets were off.

I grabbed a coffee of my own and my tablet before stepping into his office. "It's a pretty light day today. A meeting with Dan at ten, then a board meeting at two."

"You mean I actually might be able to catch up on some important things today?"

"Seems surreal, doesn't it?"

"I'm not sure I know what to do with myself."

"Well, you can start with the CS reports. The new update

launched last week, so the first week's reports should be coming in soon. Or you can work on that stack sitting on the corner of your desk."

"Why couldn't you just have said start with the top of the stack?" he asked with a groan.

I smiled at him. "Because I know you are itching to read the CS report."

"Such a tease."

I scanned my email and found something from the stack that needed his attention, and I moved around to his side. The stack was around six inches tall, with everything in its own labeled folder, which helped when looking for something specific. It was something Stacey started, and it was a fantastic idea.

"You need to sign this," I said as I pulled the folder out and opened it before placing it in front of him.

"What is it?"

"Authorization for tech to start building the platform for Chandelier. Contracts were signed and returned on Thursday."

He quickly pulled out a pen and scribbled his name before closing it up again. "I want constant updates on this one. We're trying something new for them, and I don't want any screw-ups."

"Will do," I said as I snapped a photo of the signed contract and emailed it back so they could start on it the moment they came in.

"Come closer," he said, reaching out for me.

"No," I said as I stepped back. "We need to set up some rules first."

"Rules?" he asked, his brow scrunched as he sat back.

"I'm not getting within grabbing distance of you."

"Why is that?"

"Because we have months of pent-up attraction that want to explode out in sex twenty-four seven. The problem is we have work, and the only way that is going to get done is if I keep my distance." I took a step forward, then another before falling to my knees, my hands running up his thighs until I reached his belt. "That being said, Stacey is coming in late and I thought it would be a great time for a morning treat."

He was already hard, pressed against his slacks as I worked his pants open. He stared down at me, nostrils flaring, eyes hooded, as I pulled him out.

"I think if this guy gives me a treat—" I began as I stroked his cock "—you'll be able to focus on that stack."

I braced my arms on his thighs as I gripped him with one hand, my lips closing over the tip, wetting it. I swirled my tongue around, flicking the ridge and earning a hiss before doing it again on the other side. I licked him like a lollipop because he was so big, I wasn't sure I'd ever be able to get all of it in my mouth, but I was more than willing to keep trying.

I took as much as I could, setting up a pace as I bobbed up and down. My gag reflex was the problem, but every time my throat tried to expel him, he let out a low groan that pooled heat between my thighs.

"Fuck," his head fell back on a hiss, his hand resting on my head.

His mouth was lax as his eyes bounced between watching him disappear between my lips and my eyes. He pulled the pins from my hair and shook it out before tangling his fingers in the wet strands.

I gagged hard as he held my head in place and thrust up.

"I'll train this throat," he said as his breath sped up. "You'll take it all. Down to the base."

He tensed, holding me down as he twitched, stream after stream of cum filling my mouth.

"Don't spill," he said as he slowly pulled out, the last pulses shooting even more in.

The taste wasn't bad as I swallowed, then sucked on the tip, getting the last droplets out and making him shake from over-stimulation.

"Better?" I asked as I stood, wiping my mouth off with one of the tissues in his desk drawer.

He shot up and pulled me into his arms. "My cock is still hungry," he said as he trailed kisses down my neck. "Come over tonight so I can have dessert."

"Don't I get dessert?"

"After you come on my tongue multiple times, maybe I'll give you a little cream."

I couldn't help biting down on my lower lip. Sex between us was magical. None of my past boyfriends could come close to the chemistry we had.

Later that night after dinner, Lincoln hoisted me up onto the huge center island of his kitchen. It really was a good height. His head fit perfectly between my thighs, his hands on my breasts as he devoured me. By the time he was done, I'd come multiple times and I was a pile of goo that once resembled a human, my muscles lifeless.

He came all over my stomach, giving me my dessert before carrying me into the master suite. We christened the tub, and made love until neither one of us could move.

Still, it wasn't enough.

I wanted more, and the want only grew with each time.

CHAPTER 21

Lincoln

SNAPPED UP IN BED, MY VISION STRUGGLING TO PROCESS the darkness that surrounded me. The red faded, but the shaking remained. Sweat trickled down my skin, my sheets soaked.

The nightmares were increasing.

I ran my hand over my face as I swung my legs over the edge of the bed. My heart hammered inside my chest as the vision popped before me again. I shook my head to clear it away, but it kept flashing.

Red.

Blood.

Something stirred in the bed next to me, and I jumped before flipping on the light.

There was a hiss and a groan before my eyes adjusted to the brightness. It wasn't a snake, but another creature—a siren.

Ivy's brown hair was splayed out against the white sheets, her back naked, skin flawless. Her beautiful face was nuzzled into the pillow, slender fingers hiding her eyes.

"Turn it off," she mumbled.

I stared at her, at the soft rise and fall of her chest.

After fucking for hours, we must have fallen asleep. Normally I didn't allow anyone in my place, let alone stay, but Ivy wasn't some random woman I was fucking. She was the whole package—my perfect whole package. She knew some of my deepest secrets, and knew me better than anyone.

But the darkest secrets I still kept locked away.

Guilt flooded me. An odd emotion for me, but still, it made me sick. I was using her in the worst way, and I wasn't talking about the sex.

I got up and turned off the light before using the soft light coming from the hall to guide me to the kitchen.

Ivy was going to hate me.

As my chest began to ache, I rubbed at the spot. Was that why the visions had returned? Because I was feeling more than I should?

I just had to remember the goal, the end game. It didn't matter who got hurt as long as I decimated him.

Right?

I wasn't so sure anymore.

CHAPTER 22

Lincoln
Weeks later

SENT OFF A QUICK EMAIL TO MARCUS, SENDING HIM NEW information. Every time I did, guilt nearly buried me alive. The anxiety of Ivy hating me, of hurting her in the smallest way, was crushing me.

With every email I sent via the secure site we'd been sharing information through for years, I began to wonder if, once it went down, I could just take Ivy and run away.

Money wasn't a problem, but I also didn't want to hurt the case. I'd worked for years to ruin him. To have Dante experience some fraction of the pain I felt daily when your whole world crashed down.

Dante was all about things and status and women, and destroying his company was the only way to get to him. Sending him to jail was what he deserved after what he did, but Ivy didn't deserve to be mixed up in the explosive I lit.

But there was nothing I could do. The damage was done. I

decided to be selfish, to have as much of her as I could. Treat every encounter like it could be our last and soak up every ounce of affection she showed. Every last drop of care, of love, that she showered me with.

I absorbed it all in hopes that it would carry me through, but I had no idea when or where the other side was, or if she'd even be there.

It took a week and a very long weekend spent in bed for my lust for her to settle down enough that I wasn't constantly pawing at her in the office. Months of pent-up need couldn't be stopped once the invisible wall that held me back was gone. She'd spent the entire week at my place as we gorged on each other.

No matter how much I fucked her, how many times I came inside her, the insatiable lust never waned. It only grew stronger until I had her morning, noon, and night. Then mid-afternoon and sometime around midnight popped in.

I couldn't stop fucking her.

I didn't want to stop.

Driven by the pleasure. Chasing the inevitable high that never seemed to last as long as the time before.

I couldn't remember a time when I wanted a woman as much as I wanted Ivy. It was a bone-deep-need, and every day my feelings expanded while the guilt hung heavier around my neck, dragging me down.

"What's on the agenda for this afternoon?" I asked as Ivy stood in front of me. I was still sitting in my chair, rocking back and staring at her.

The morning had been full of meetings and I was ready for a break, but that desire started to crawl in as I stared at her legs, imagining them locked around my hips, locked around my head. I wanted to pull her down to her knees, to have her take me into her mouth, but there was only twenty minutes until I was meeting Koa for lunch.

Still, I couldn't stop from scooting my chair closer and running my fingers along the side and backs of her legs.

"You have…" She drew in a ragged breath when my hands moved further up and pulled her closer.

Everything told me to take her, that nothing mattered but having her.

"L-Lincoln," she stuttered as I drew her skirt up.

What would one taste hurt?

I pulled her thong to the side before leaning in and swiping my tongue across her clit. A groan left me as I dug in, my mouth devouring her pussy, spurred on by her fingers fisting my hair and the moans she tried to stifle.

The intern, whatever her name was, still sat outside, and I gave no shits if she heard. I had one focus, and that was Ivy exploding on my tongue.

I dug my fingers into her ass, pulling her closer. By the pitch of her voice she was growing closer while I grew harder.

Fuck it. I needed to be inside her.

I removed one hand from her and unbuttoned my pants to free my aching cock. As soon as it cleared my zipper, I released my mouth and pulled on her hips, settling her onto my lap.

Confusion filled her eyes, but the moment I slid inside her they rolled back.

An electric pulse shot through me as her warmth surrounded me. It felt better, closer than before. Every thought left me as pleasure took control, driving my movements.

"That's it, baby," I whispered into her ear as I guided her along my length, my hips flexing up. "I want you to come around me."

Wordlessly, she wrapped her arms around my shoulders and rested her forehead against mine as she worked her hips.

"Take it."

Her lips brushed against mine and I tilted my head, capturing them, my tongue immediately lapping against hers. I held her tighter, my cock pistoning in and out of her like my life depended on it.

Every thrust drove us both closer until I felt her freeze in my arms, her mouth opening as a stifled, high-pitch moan left her.

"Come on my cock." I never let up, my cock working her as her orgasm rocked her in my arms.

The pulsation of her walls became too much. I reached my limit, my balls drawn up, and slammed her down as I pushed up, exploding deep inside her.

I relaxed back and we sat there, both breathing hard and boneless.

When the fog cleared, a nagging in the back of my mind came to light as I stared up at the ceiling.

"I just came in you," I said in a rush.

She nodded against my shoulder. "So full."

"Without a condom."

"Mmm hmm."

"Should I not be freaking out?"

She shook her head and sat back. "Birth control."

I blinked at her. "I can come in you?" How did I not know that before? Probably because I was used to wearing a condom. It'd been a decade since I'd last had a steady girlfriend, so I protected myself from disease and pregnancies.

She bit down on her lip and smiled. "Whenever you want."

A groan left me. "Don't say that."

"Why?"

"Because it is difficult enough to keep away from you for an hour. Now I'll never be able to pull my cock out of you again."

"That's a bad thing?" she asked.

Such a little minx. She tried again and again to act all business like, that she wasn't as affected, but more than once she'd pounced on me after a meeting. The small conference table in my office had been officially broken in due to her.

"Well, we have work and such," I reminded her. "We can't just stay in bed all day," I said, mimicking what she'd said to me before.

"Why not?"

I groaned against her throat, my teeth nipping at her skin. "Don't tempt me."

"All I did was start going over the agenda."

"You were within ten feet of me. You know you can't do that without me getting worked up."

"You, sir, need to get a little self-control."

"I've been pretty good," I argued. Over the past few weeks, usually after hours, but sometimes not, we worked on making sure every square inch of my office was tainted. However, my desk was still my favorite spot. There was something about having her there that was both erotic and exciting. We were spending most nights with each other. Sometimes at her place, but more often at mine. Both Austin and my breakfast delivery service were confused from day to day.

"If by pretty good you mean acting like a horny teenager, then yes."

"I'm not that bad." Yes, yes, I was. Something about Ivy I couldn't get enough. Not enough of her body or her mind. I soaked her in, and still I was never full.

It was a desperation for her that was driven by the impending end of us. Every day I clung harder to her, begging for just one more day.

I let out a hiss as her hips rose while resisting the urge to grab her and pull her back down. Her warmth was gone, my dick out in the cool air. Pearl droplets fell onto my pants, and I let out a groan as I stared at her well-fucked slit.

I couldn't explain the primal pride I felt seeing my cum dripping from her.

"Don't look at me like that," she chastised me.

"I can't stare at your beauty?"

"No, you can't stare at me like you want to go again. I know that look."

A chuckle left me. She was right, and she had seen it many times before.

"Besides, you need to get cleaned up for lunch with your sister."

"Shit." I tucked my dick back in my pants before moving to the bathroom. A quick rinse off, check of my clothes, a spray of cologne, and I was ready.

"Better?" I asked as I stepped out.

Ivy drew in a deep breath from her nose, stepping closer until she was pressed against me, drawing in another deep breath.

"I love your cologne." Her fingers moved down, passing my belt and cupping me.

"Weren't you just saying how I needed to leave?"

"Hmm? Leave?"

"The sooner I have lunch with her, the sooner you get to meet her," I reminded her as I moved away. "I'll be back."

"Have a good lunch," she said with a wave.

There was no doubt Dakota would like Ivy, but I needed to talk to her, face to face, before they met. I was caught in the trap of wanting them to meet and not wanting them to meet because my time with Ivy was limited.

Austin was waiting for me outside the front doors, and we were able to make it without being too far behind. Still, Dakota was waiting for me when I sat down on the patio of the restaurant.

"Sorry I'm late," I said.

She stared at me for a moment, eyeing me. "Who are you and what have you done with my brother?"

"Excuse me?"

"You're like, happy or something."

"Kind of."

She continued to stare at me, concentrating like she was trying to read my mind. "You're fucking a girl. A girl you actually like."

"How do you know?" I asked in complete surprise.

"You have that 'I got laid' shit-eating grin I've seen on way too many guys before. The difference is I'm not sure I've ever seen you smile so much, at least not since, you know, *before*."

If I saw a therapist, they would probably call what we were doing repression or something. Dakota and I didn't talk about it. Try as she might, my baby sister just couldn't fill the void of my twin. Still, I could never repay her for staying in Seattle with me.

"Well, *before*, I was a completely different person," I reminded her.

"True."

The waiter came by and took our drink orders before disappearing. The food looked good, and I was starving. As I glanced at all the options, I was secretly happy she wasn't with us because there was no way she would let me have many of the items that caught my eye.

"So, how's the revenge game going?"

"Progress."

"I sense a but."

I let the menu fall back to the table. "But the girl is tied up in it."

"You like her a lot, don't you?"

I let out a sigh. "Very much. Too much."

"Are you going to hurt her?" she asked.

It struck me in the chest, because while I knew what I was doing, nobody had asked me. Marcus told me, but when Dakota asked, it was like a punch to the gut.

I nodded. "It's gone too far at this point. I can't stop it." I rubbed the back of my knuckles against my chest. "Jesus, Koa, why did you have to remind me?"

"Because reality is a fucking bitch." She slapped her hands down on the table. "Don't you see the irony here? You're going to hurt a girl in order to get revenge on Dante."

"He's the reason—"

"I know, I know. Trust me, I'm your biggest supporter outside of Mom and Dad in this whole scheme, but this woman you care about is an innocent. She's going to be collateral damage. When the dust settles, what then?"

I shook my head. "I don't know."

"Typical one-track mind. You have this plan, and you act out the plan with no care for those on the sidelines. She's going to hate you, and you're still going to be a miserable fuck!"

I slammed my hand down on the table. "I know! Fuck, Koa, you think I don't know, that I don't think about it? From the first moment I met her, I knew."

"You knew you were going to sacrifice her, but you didn't know you were going to sacrifice yourself."

Dakota may not have been my other half, but she was still my sister, and still very capable of calling me out on my shit. She knew me, knew my secrets, knew my pain, and knew just how to twist the knife.

"I never planned to hurt anyone," I told her.

"I know, but you will." She sat back and let out a sigh. "I've already lost my sister, Linc. I don't want to lose my brother as well."

"That won't happen," I assured her.

"What's your plan, then?" she asked as the waiter set down our drinks. We still needed a few minutes as we'd barely looked at the menu, and he disappeared again.

"I don't know, but I'll figure it out," I replied as soon as he was gone.

With her index finger, she tapped on the watch that sat on her wrist. London's watch. "Tick-tock, big brother."

"How are the wedding plans coming?" I asked.

She held up her hand. "Hold on, I need to buckle my seatbelt for the ninety-degree right turn you just took."

My lip twitched. "Smart-ass."

She blew out a breath, the smile gone from her face. "I love you, Linc, and I hope one day you can move past this and be happy. I just want to see you happy again."

Ivy makes me happy.

I didn't say the words out loud because it would only remind me of the vicious cycle I'd inadvertently created. I only hoped that when the dust settled Ivy would be able to forgive me. That she would understand.

That she could love me enough to love me after.

CHAPTER 23

Ivy

WAS NAKED, BREATHING HARD, AND SWEATING WHILE thinking about whether or not I really needed that gym membership when every day and night I got a vigorous workout with Lincoln.

"What were we doing for dinner?" he asked as he propped himself up on his elbow.

"Food."

A deep chuckle echoed in his chest. "Mexican? Italian? Steak? Chicken? Waffles?"

I quirked a brow at him. "Waffles?"

He shrugged. "Breakfast for dinner."

"I could go for a breakfast sandwich and some home fries."

"That does sound good."

His fingers traveled along the path of my necklace, my breath hitching the lower they traveled to where the end rested between my breasts. Was he ready to go again already?

"You wear this every day," he said, his fingers running back up the chain.

"You noticed."

His mouth drew up into a smirk. "Only took me seeing you in nothing but a necklace for a month."

"So perceptive, Mr. Devereux."

"Don't take that for me not seeing it all, because you are a spectacular vision in nothing. I just hadn't noticed it was the same one every day. Present from another man?"

A laugh left me, making him scowl at me. Lincoln showing even the slightest bit of jealousy was so cute.

"It was a gift from Iris before I moved to Seattle."

"Tiffany?" he asked as he noted the inscription on one of the hearts.

I nodded. "I don't remember how or why. I think it was shortly after Mom died and they opened a location in the Fashion Mall, which is the expensive mall in Indianapolis. For some reason we were enamored with those little blue boxes. I think it was because it reminded us of her and better times. Dad had given her a bracelet from there the Christmas before she got sick. But from that moment, we wanted something, anything from there. It didn't matter what was on the inside. So, when we graduated and I was packing up to move, I got a see-you-later gift for her. A little blue box." A smile grew, and I ran my finger down the chain slipped through one of the hearts and it dangled another heart a few inches lower. "We laughed so hard when Iris pulled one out too. Of course, by then, it was obvious what was on the inside was exactly the same."

"You light up so much when you talk about Iris." He played with the lower heart, twirling it between his fingers. "London and I had something similar. I got her a watch for our eighteenth birthday, had it engraved with 'you are my sunshine.'"

He let out a chuckle. "She used to always hum that song, and it became my nickname for her. That same birthday, she got me a watch as well."

He pulled up his arm to reveal a large watch that was still in good shape, which meant he not only took care of it, but it was also probably stainless steel. It amazed me that eighteen years had passed and he still wore it every day.

"It's engraved with 'my only sunshine.'"

My heart broke once again. They were as close as Iris and me, and he lost that.

"What happened to hers?" I asked.

"She wore it until the day she died. Koa wears it now."

Lincoln rubbed his hand across his mouth and down his jaw. There was a wetness in his eyes, and I reached up to cup his face, my thumb caressing his cheek. He leaned into my palm and kissed it.

I hadn't met the infamous Koa, a.k.a. Dakota Devereux, but I wanted to. Especially after he fessed up that all the gifts I was sending out in my early days of working for him were actually going to her.

"You don't talk about London very much." As hard as it was for him to talk about her, I knew it was good for him. He needed the release for all the pain he'd stuffed down.

He shook his head. "It's difficult."

I pulled him close, resting his head on my shoulder, and stroked his hair. He nuzzled into my neck, his arms wrapping around my waist and pulling me closer.

"What was she like?" I asked, just wanting to hear more about her.

"She was the sun. Bright and shining every day. So full of joy and beauty and selflessness. Nobody but me knew the dark that would swallow her up."

"Because it would swallow you up, too?"

He nodded. "Yes."

"Briar used to be a big jerk. He would always pinch one of us hard while the other was somewhere else to see if we felt it. No matter how many times we told him that wasn't how it worked, even though it did."

"Who is Briar?"

Whoops. Hadn't I told Lincoln his name before? "My brother."

Lincoln lifted his head, his brow furrowed. "Wait, your brother's name is Briar? Like a briar patch?"

I nodded. "It fits his personality, too."

"Ivy, Iris, Briar… Are your parents horticulturists?"

I let out a laugh. "Actually, my mom was."

"You don't talk much about her."

I shrugged. "She fought cancer, and cancer won." It was hard to believe twelve years had passed. "I miss her every day, but she's still with me, in here." I tapped my chest, right over my heart as I fought back the tears filling my eyes. "And I know she's looking down on us and is proud of how we turned out."

"Do you think London is? Do you think she found peace?"

I swallowed hard, trying to hold back the tears, my chest burning, keeping a sob at bay. I failed at the tears when one slid down my temple. His pain was tearing my heart out.

"I'm sure she is, and one day you'll see her again." I drew in a steadying breath, my fingers playing with his hair while his made lazy circles around my ribs. "What about you?"

"What about me?"

"Lincoln, London, and Dakota?"

"That. Well, my father is from South Dakota, my mother

from Lincoln, Nebraska, and they met while doing a semester in London."

Thankfully the mood started to lighten. "See, I'm not the only family with a weird way of deciding names."

"True."

"What if there had been a fourth Devereux?"

"Probably Colorado or Denver, even though we didn't live in Denver."

All the name talk had me thinking about something I never thought about—children. I wasn't ready, but I felt like I was with my future. That maybe one day we would have a family, maybe even twins. Would we name them like our parents named us?

He blew out a breath and sat up, stretching over me to pick his phone up from the nightstand.

"What was the verdict on dinner?" he asked as he pulled up the restaurant app.

"Breakfast."

"Right."

I stared at him as he searched through the list of possible restaurants, at his angular jaw with a day's worth of scruff. Slowly but surely, we were getting to know each other on a level neither of us was used to. Deeper and fuller in the knowledge of one another, knowledge that few knew.

As I admired him a different kind of warmth blossomed in my chest. He was so handsome, and I felt so lucky to call him mine.

∽

Stacey was at lunch when Lincoln and I arrived back from a meeting. Almost as soon as we made it through the glass doors, the phone began to ring.

"Let it go to voicemail," Lincoln said, already starting to get handsy.

I turned to him and smiled. "I don't know if my boss would appreciate that." I reached over my desk and picked the phone up from the receiver. "Lincoln Devereux's office."

"Are you happy?" It took me a second to process the voice.

"Dante?" At the name, Lincoln's head snapped to me.

"You left with barely a goodbye, ran to *him*, started fucking *him* when you wouldn't give me the time of day," Dante spat, his words stumbling a bit the way they did when he'd been drinking. "Do you think he's better than me?"

"Yes," I said coolly.

Laughter filled my ears, harsh and full of anger. "You did it on purpose, you bitch."

"Excuse me?" He wasn't making sense.

"You're a fucking *bitch*, Ivy!"

I didn't have time to react or respond, because Lincoln heard. He snatched the phone from my hand, his jaw set, eyes full of fire. "Do you talk to your mother like that, you piece of shit?... That's your problem... Are you drunk?... Why are you calling here? ... Ivy? She has done nothing. Listen... Listen... Look, you goddamn son of a bitch," he growled into the phone, his body shaking in anger. "Don't ever call here again. Ivy doesn't work for you, she works for me... Consider it karma, you narcissistic ass... Stop harassing my employees... Go to hell," he spat, his jaw locked tight as he raged. "In fact, I hope you end up in the fiery pits with constant torture every second of eternity. You deserve nothing less."

Lincoln slammed the receiver back into the cradle. He was breathing hard, his nostrils flared.

"What was that?" I asked after a few beats of silence. I'd been frozen in complete shock at his reaction.

With a strong tug he pulled on the phone, yanking it from its anchor in the wall, and threw it down on the floor. He stared at it, then proceeded to stomp on it.

I was transfixed by the uncharacteristic violence he was exuding. Frightened not by him, but by the darkness Dante brought out in him. There was more than hatred between them. Something darker with the power to transform Lincoln.

"Lincoln?"

At the sound of his name, his head snapped to me, the anger melted, and he rushed around the desk and pulled me into his arms.

"He can't take you from me."

"Hey, shh." I held him close as I attempted to process what had just transpired. I could only hear Lincoln's side of the conversation, and I didn't understand why he said any of it. I knew there was bad blood between them, but Lincoln's reaction was beyond that of a minor feud.

There were more secrets he hadn't shared, so much I still didn't know, but one day I would, when he was ready. That secret I could wait for.

It took almost half an hour to calm him down, my usual tactics lacking their effectiveness when I was caged in his arms on his lap. He wouldn't let me go, and I began to become concerned when he finally let out a long breath and started to relax.

"Are you okay?" I asked as I brushed the hair from his forehead. The tiredness in his eyes wasn't there this morning, but after Dante called, they were dull and heavy.

"I apologize for scaring you," he said softly. His eyes closed, his head falling back as my fingers absently played with his hair.

"That feels good."

The desire to ask him, to pull the information I wanted from him, was strong, but he was in no shape to have that kind of conversation. I wanted to know what happened between them. How deep was their history, why so much hatred? I thought it was a simple rivalry with anger about stealing clients and trying to be the top company, but now I saw it ran much deeper.

"Why?" I asked. It just flew out, an open-ended question that I had no clue what the answer would be.

His eyes met mine. "He's the only person who can set me off like that."

I nodded. "You get angry sometimes, but nothing to that extent."

He ran his hand up and down the outside of my thigh as he stared out the window, his brow furrowed.

"Remember how once you said when he was drunk he kept saying 'we' in regards to a software he sold?"

"Yes."

"I am the other half of that we."

I froze and stared at him. "W-what?"

"He stole it, moved to Seattle, and sold it."

My mind was racing, whirling around trying to figure it out. "How? How is that even legal?"

"Because he is a conniving snake, which is why I was surprised that he hadn't protected himself with a non-compete clause when he hired you. Then again, his ego, his narcissistic personality would never allow him to believe you'd leave him for me."

"As much as he wanted, he never had me," I reminded him.

His fingertips brushed against my cheek and pushed my

hair back behind my ear. "But I do, and he's always wanted what I have."

"Well, he can't ever have me."

Those tortured eyes stared back at me, the ones that still held secrets, but also pain. "No. You're mine."

And I was.

∞

For the rest of the afternoon, Lincoln stayed in his head. He didn't talk, didn't call me into his office. He didn't act like Lincoln.

I still couldn't believe it, that Dante had done something so horrible. He made millions off that sale, and I don't think Lincoln ever saw a penny. No wonder he was so driven to be the best, to topple Kilgore. It all made sense. Trust was broken, which was why he didn't really have any friends. It also explained some of our issues in the beginning.

Their feud wasn't a feud at all, but an all-out war, one that Lincoln was winning. He'd made DCS the premier client database software and storage company in the country. When he'd taken over, Kilgore was the rising giant, but karma was a bitch, after all.

"Ivy, can you come here," Lincoln's voice called from inside his office.

I grabbed my tablet and walked in.

"Yes?"

"I need you to clear the schedule for next week."

"Sir?"

"As you know we've been trying to break into the international market. I have some contacts in Rome who wants to talk but only if it's in person, and I want you to come with me."

I blinked at him. "What?"

"Come with me to Rome."

"To Rome?" I repeated, trying to figure out a Rome other than the one in Italy.

"Yes. I was thinking we can work, take a few days off to look around, and then come home."

"A workcation?"

He nodded. "Somewhat. Though the days we're looking around are just for Lincoln and Ivy."

A smile grew on my face and I reached out for his hand. "I'd like that."

He took my hand and lightly pressed his lips to my knuckles. "Same."

We spent the remainder of the day ironing out the details, finding a hotel and flights.

Excitement had me bouncing in my chair like a child waiting for a sweet. For years I'd dreamed of seeing other countries, of traveling the world, but it always seemed out of reach. There was never time, even when I did have the money. I'd had my passport for years, having made a few trips to Vancouver which I didn't exactly count as leaving the country.

Lincoln insisted we fly first class, and even tried to flirt with the idea of the mile-high club.

It was exactly what he needed to get him out of the funk created by Dante, and I was excited for my first vacation ever with a boyfriend.

CHAPTER 24

Lincoln

THE FIRST NIGHT IN ROME, I FUCKED IVY TO SLEEP JUST before midnight. The nine-hour time difference was a beast, but when we awoke in the morning, there was no jet lag.

She worked perfectly by my side. Symphony at its finest, leaving me in awe at her even more than normal. On the first night, the client took us to dinner as we talked more, and by the end, they were impressed and ready to sign on the dotted line.

The credit was due a lot to Ivy. She was personable and knew all the right things to say—a true right-hand woman.

A true queen.

There were tourist adventures, neither of us having been to Italy before. We took trips to the Colosseum and the Forum, along with the Vatican and St. Peters. The taste of Italian pizza outweighed anything I'd ever had in the States. It was completely different, just as New York-style and Chicago-style were a class of their own. The trip was like a dream, and I didn't want to go back to reality.

I brushed my fingers through her hair as her head rested on my chest, a low hum, almost purr-like, coming from her with each stroke.

"This was fabulous," she said. "Do we have to go back?"

I pressed my lips against the top of her head. "Sadly."

"We couldn't stay longer? I'm really liking all this time with my boyfriend."

A bolt of heat shot straight into my chest, and I froze.

Boyfriend.

We hadn't labeled us, even after well over a month, and I hadn't given her a title to anyone other than introducing her as my assistant, but it didn't make it any less true—Ivy was my girlfriend.

How long had it been since I was last in a relationship? Ten years? Even I wasn't sure. I'd been so focused on revenge for so long that there was no room for anything else.

"Lincoln?"

I looked down to find her looking up at me. "Hmm?"

"You froze."

"I was just thinking."

"About?" she asked, a nervous edge to her voice.

I brushed a lock of hair from her face and stared into her eyes. "If I've ever felt anything like this before."

"Like this?"

A chuckle left me. "Stop fishing."

"Seriously, what do you feel?"

What I felt wasn't something I was able to put into words. My emotions were strong, but laced with the coming tragedy that I tried so hard to forget. "So much, too much. Being with you is scary, but as easy as breathing. Everything about you is everything I'd forgotten I wanted. I was focused on one thing for so long that I didn't look at the world or the future anymore, only at the finish line. You mend the pieces, put me back together, make me a man again, and you do it effortlessly."

She tucked her head into my neck. "You make me out to be something so much more than I am."

"You're Beauty, and I'm the Beast." It really was a good analogy for our situation.

"You're no beast," she said as her fingers made lazy circles on my chest.

"I can be."

"Yes, well, anyone can be," she argued.

I cupped her cheek and turned her to face me. "He had one target and watched it fall away, fade until he was forever a beast, but then a beauty came and reminded him what it was like to live, to be human again. You're my Belle, Ivy."

Her bottom lip trembled, her brow scrunched, and her eyes began to water. "Don't say that unless you mean it."

"I mean every word," I assured her as I stroked her cheek with my thumb. "Since the first moment you slammed into me, I haven't stopped thinking about you. Just like the plant you're named after, you took hold and wouldn't let go."

"I'll never let you go," she whispered.

I couldn't help but chuckle. "You know that sounds a little creepy."

"Didn't Rose say something like that to Jack in *Titanic?*"

"And?"

"It was romantic there," she said.

I shook my head. "Until he was a popsicle and she let him go."

"What I'm saying is, despite your earlier behavior, it was the same for me. From the first moment you grabbed me to stop my fall, there was something there. That touch was like a promise, a taste of what could be."

"The beginning wasn't easy," I reminded her.

"If it's easy, it's not as sweet."

"How so?" I asked.

She sat up and looked down at me, my hand falling back down, caressing her breast as it went. "We worked hard to get here, denying our physical attraction while we got to know one another in the highest tension environment possible."

She was right, but not for the same reason. I didn't want to get into the situation I was going to be put in, but I just couldn't stay away. Ivy had become my life force.

"It happened because you said you didn't want more than a professional relationship."

"Huge effort on my part to say that, because all I wanted was for you to kiss me like that again. At the time, I was so attracted to you, but our personalities were still battling things out. I hoped that once the dust faded from that, if I was still attracted to you it was more than a crush or a fling."

"Are you not so attracted to me anymore?"

"Fishing? All right. Mr. Devereux, I am so attracted to you that it took everything in me to refrain from straddling you on that airplane."

I pulled her closer, wishing I could pull her inside me. All I wanted was to protect her. "Every moment I'm near you, it takes every ounce of strength to not pull you into my arms. You have no idea how hard that was in the beginning."

"Don't hold back."

"Never again." I ghosted my lips against hers before pressing hard.

Thousands of miles from home on a bed with a view

overlooking the most beautiful city I had ever seen, I held my perfect woman in my arms. A vision I couldn't live without. I cupped her breathtaking face and pulled her closer, settling between her thighs to make love until we couldn't move.

Ivy was perfection, a goddess in mortal form. She was everything I'd ever wanted and would ever want. All of those wants were morphing into necessity.

I couldn't do it. Giving her up was no longer possible. There had to be a way, and I was going to find it.

I would fight heaven and hell to keep her beside me.

It hit me then.

Fuck.

I'm in love with Ivy.

CHAPTER 25

Ivy

L EAVING ROME WAS SAD. I NEVER KNEW THAT I COULD BE so happy, that I could feel as loved as Lincoln made me feel. My heart had wings and was soaring high in the sky.

It was a euphoric high. The type that made me feel invincible with him by my side, because nobody felt safer or more right. Lincoln was absolutely amazing. It was something I already knew, but the days away where we could truly spend as just Ivy and Lincoln were a dream.

From romantic dinners to holding hands while we went sightseeing to nights lavishing my body with attention, he was proving himself to be the god I'd imagined.

"You are too delicious," Lincoln said as he stepped up behind me.

Coming back to work was hard, especially since I'd had to go home the night before. It was the first night in weeks that we'd spent apart, and solely due to the trip and the need to unpack and get fresh clothing. The moment his hands touched me, the heat in the room doubled. How were we ever supposed to work again when we were totally and completely consumed with each other?

"Don't let my boyfriend hear you say that," I said.

A low growl vibrated in his chest as he pulled me against him, his lips finding mine.

Kissing him was like coming home—warm and inviting. Every single time. Away from him seemed cold and lonely, but in his arms was where I was meant to be.

We were brought together by so many factors, and I had no doubt the fates were one of those. From the time he'd lost London, his soul had cried out for me. It guided me to Seattle, and the path that led me to him.

I loved Lincoln with every fiber of my being. Somehow, that didn't scare me. Not anymore, because it felt so right.

"Hi," I said when he pulled back just enough for a breath.

His lip twitched up, his hands circling around my back. "Hi."

"Can we go back?" I asked against his lips.

"Yes."

"Now?"

He chuckled. "No, not now, but soon."

"How soon is soon?"

"We could go on a European tour," he said, his tone more serious than I was expecting.

I let out a sigh as I stepped out of his arms and did the difficult task of making space. "I wish."

"Where do you think you're going?" Lincoln asked as he took hold of my arm and pulled me back into him.

A laugh left me as I wrapped my arms around his neck. "We have that work thing, remember? Meetings and such."

"Fuck them."

"Fuck them?"

His eyes flickered between mine as he hands massaged against my back as they worked their way down. "All I want to do is everything we should have done in my bed last night."

"You could have come to my place."

His hands flexed against my ass. "I want to come *in* your place."

I shook my head. "You're terrible."

"You make me this way." He leaned down and kissed my cheek.

"So, I'm to blame?"

"Very much so."

"And why is that?" I asked, loving the playful side of him.

"Because you are too addictive for your own good. You make me a monster for you."

"I like it when you're a monster."

"Why is that?"

I pulled my lips between my teeth as I drew my hands up into his hair. "Because that want you exude is so intoxicating, I can't concentrate on anything but you."

"Good." He slammed his lips against mine, not holding back in the least as he attempted to devour me, and I loved every second of it.

How did I get so lucky? I wanted his touch to never end, and for him to never let me go.

"I see you are a slut after all, huh Ivy?" a very familiar voice called out.

Both of us snapped our heads toward the voice, the heat suddenly doused in ice water at the view of the man before us.

Dante didn't resemble the man I'd last seen. His hair and

clothes were unkempt, his pallor resembling a man who'd been drinking himself to death for days. He looked unsteady and no longer the cocky, smooth-talking womanizer I knew him to be.

What had happened to him?

CHAPTER 26

Lincoln

DREAD SETTLED INTO MY STOMACH THE SECOND I HEARD his voice, cold and weighted like a hundred-ton stone. One look, and I knew why he was there. He looked like a zombie, a dead man walking in the truest sense and I knew it was the end, but I had trouble accepting it.

I said I was going to find a way, but my time was suddenly gone. A small handful of hours had passed since I became determined to keep her, but my minutes had dissolved, my seconds erased.

No. I can't.

I wasn't ready to let Ivy go. I never wanted to let her go. Ever.

But I had no choice. Not anymore. Keeping her as close to me as possible was the opposite of what was good for her, because I failed.

My grip tightened on her waist, soaking in one last feel of her in my arms before I pushed her away and turned on the vile man who had somehow entered the executive floor.

"Watch what you fucking say to her, Dante," I growled.

His glare turned to me, and I got a look at just how unhinged he'd become. His eyes were wild, and it was obvious he was hanging on by a thread.

"Or what? Gonna turn me in for some other stupid infraction?"

I wasn't prepared. I knew it was coming sometime, but why didn't Marcus warn me? "Embezzlement isn't stupid, and your shareholders should know. It's only one of the laws you've broken."

He stepped toward Ivy, whose eyes went wide. "You did this, didn't you? You ungrateful bitch!"

I moved between them, jaw locked as I shot daggers at him with my eyes. "One more word, and I won't hesitate to lay you out."

"You couldn't beat me at twenty, what makes you think you'll beat me now?"

"Incentive." Every fiber of my being begged for him to take me up on it, to have some release for years of pain.

"I'm calling security," Ivy said from behind me. Her hand left my back as she retreated to her desk.

"You fucked me over," Dante spat as he watched her closely.

"You fucked yourself over. This is all a product of *your* actions, nobody else." I looked back to Ivy, who was staring back as she spoke into the receiver.

"That again? It's been years, Lincoln, and it wasn't my fault," he said.

My whole body went rigid, and I slowly turned back toward him. "What did you say?"

"I said it wasn't my fault. I had nothing to do with it."

I couldn't stop myself. I reached out, grabbed onto his shirt, and spun him, slamming him against the wall.

"You had *everything* to do with it. *Everything.*"

He managed to push me off, and I didn't see his fist coming at me until I was looking somewhere else, pain radiating through my face.

"Like I said, Lincoln, you couldn't beat me—"

I didn't let him finish, and took my turn to slam my fist into his face. For years I'd punched a boxing dummy imagining it was him, and the crunch of his flesh beneath my blow was so much more cathartic.

As soon as he was upright, he lunged at me but missed. My tightly balled fist connected with his stomach at the same time his other hand whipped back around, landing squarely on my jaw. The hit I delivered had him bent over, holding his stomach. Just as he was straightening, I toppled him with one last strike.

Writhing on the ground was too good for him. He needed to be buried beneath it.

In the back of my mind a familiar voice called out to me, but I was too focused on the man in front of me to comprehend. For years I'd imagined the day I brought him down, delivered some amount of justice for what he did to me.

"Lincoln!" Ivy called out. It was strong enough and for a second, I glanced over to the woman I loved. Her beautiful eyes were full of worry, and I breathed in their love one last time.

It was a beat too long, allowing Dante to rise and charge at me. His shoulder dug into my chest as he slammed me against the wall. The breath flew from my lungs, and I braced for the next hit while I aimed my own.

But they didn't come. Strong hands grabbed and pulled us apart. Security had arrived, and they brought friends.

The Seattle PD had arrived as well.

I was breathing hard as I watched them cuff him. Pain began to soak in as the adrenaline left me. More places hurt than blows I remembered receiving, but then again, I was focused on landing my own.

The officers took statements, all the while the pain migrated and settled in my heart. As soon as the officer stepped away, my heart cracked.

Fuck. It's here. It's time.

I hated Dante even more in that moment. Yes, it was my plan, but he was why it was initiated and now it was costing me Ivy.

I was going to keep her safe, keep her out of this, no matter what, but I never prepared my heart.

Ivy.

My love.

Please forgive me one day for what I am about to do.

Her worried blue eyes found mine before she rushed over. I wanted to thrash him all over again for making me do it, but it was the only way.

"Lincoln, your face," Ivy said as she reached up.

I grabbed hold of her hands before she could touch me, and stepped back. If she touched me, really touched me, I wouldn't be able to. "Get out."

Her brow furrowed as she looked at me in confusion. "What?"

The whole situation made me angry, and I channeled that rage. I'd found happiness for the first time in years, and I was going to destroy it of my own volition.

"I told you I was going to hurt you. I warned you, but like any other lost puppy, you hung onto me, onto every word, so listen to me now." I stared deep into her eyes that were so confused, pulling up all of my hatred I could in order to get the job done. "I used you, Ivy. I used your affection, your soft heart, your gullibility. And now, I don't need you anymore. I got what I wanted."

"Lincoln, I don't understand."

I let out a dark laugh. "Of course you don't. You weren't a queen. You were nothing but a pawn in my game. I got what I needed from you, information on Dante, and now I don't need you. *You're fired*," I sneered. "Grab your things. There's the door. Use it now before I call security to remove you."

Tears filled her eyes as absolute confusion and hurt filled her expression.

"Lincoln—"

"Get. Out!" I yelled.

That made her jump, and she scurried away, glancing back at me. So much turmoil.

I stayed strong, kept the anger on the surface while my heart was breaking.

"And you called me a cold-hearted son of a bitch. Look what you just did," Dante spat as the officers picked him up from the floor.

"Don't ever compare yourself to me again." I forced myself not to look at her as she paused at the glass door, and used only my periphery. "Have fun rotting in jail."

He shook his head. "This isn't over, Lincoln. I'll fucking get you."

I leaned in and whispered in his ear. "Karma is a bitch."

I should have enjoyed watching them cart him away, but the tsunami of pain was rushing forward. While my queen's information may have provided the check make on the black king, I toppled my own kingdom in the process.

As soon as he was out the door, I waged a new war, this time on anything in my office. Nothing was safe from my warpath as I tossed chairs, toppled tables, and broke every piece of anything before me.

When the dust settled and I sat in exhaustion in the wake of my devastation, I had to ask myself one question.

Was it worth it?

CHAPTER 27

Ivy

WALKING IN THE DOOR OF MY APARTMENT, I WAS IN A daze. I didn't even know how I got home. I made the drive on autopilot, and I was shocked that my car seemed to be intact, but that was more than I could say for myself.

A haze of confusion and sorrow had washed over me, clouding everything. Didn't we just get back from a fairy tale trip to Rome? Didn't we just tell one another how deep our feelings had become?

Never had I felt so strongly about another person other than Iris.

I was like a mindless zombie, still too stunned to comprehend what had happened. One minute I was stupid in love having just returned from the most romantic trip imaginable, and the next...

Everything was over. The man I thought I knew threw me out without a second glance.

What happened? I was lost, unable to make heads or tails

out of what had taken place in his office.

Dante was there being the bastard he was, Lincoln defended me, but then suddenly the world went sideways.

He dismissed me. Harshly. Permanently.

The man I loved told me how he used me to get to Dante, that I was nothing but a pawn.

I sat staring at the blank television, my reflection staring back at me with the stunned pain I felt in her eyes. The idea to pinch myself to see if it was all a dream was strong, but the pain in my chest and the difficulty breathing was more powerful than any pinch.

I had no idea how much time had passed when the ringing of my phone dragging me out of my frozen state.

"Hello?"

"Ivy, there you are," Alex said with a sigh of relief. "I've been calling your desk phone but you weren't answering. What's going on?"

"I…I don't really know."

"There were cops, and now the feds are here. Dante Kilgore was taken out in handcuffs. One second you were here, and the next you're not, and all this shit is going on. What happened?"

What did happen? What happened to my loving boyfriend?

"I have no clue. I just know I got fired." There was no intonation in my voice. Flat, as devoid of emotion as I was.

"Fired? That's crazy! Why would you get fired?"

"That's what I want to know."

"But you're his girlfriend," she said, her tone rising as it faded.

"Not anymore. He said he used me and said he was done, and that was it." My heart cracked. It had to be a lie, a play.

That thought was the only thing that kept me from completely falling apart.

"Oh, my God. That's awful! What's your address? I'm coming over."

"Thank you, Alex, but I think I just want to be alone right now."

"Tomorrow?"

"Okay," I said to placate her. "I'll text you my address."

"Please call me if you need anything. I don't care what time it is and how trivial you think it is, call me."

"Thank you," I said as I pulled the phone away and ended the call. I really was grateful for her friendship, but I wasn't up for visitors and a million questions for which I had no answers.

I didn't want to talk to anyone but Lincoln, and I didn't want to believe what he said. So, I waited.

I couldn't eat, couldn't sleep, nor did I move. I just sat there on my couch waiting for some word from him, but the phone never rang, and when light filtered over the horizon, I knew he wasn't coming.

The sun rising wasn't the start of a new day, but the end of the most beautiful thing I'd experienced in my life. It was the first day without Lincoln in my life. The first day without love.

The sun lifted, and all the pain I'd held back flooded in. It felt like I was drowning. Waves crashing over me, pummeling me, keeping me from the surface.

I let him in, fell head over heels for him, and let him use me. When he was done, he was done with me.

Tears flowed like rivers down my cheeks, and my bottom lip trembled. The phone rang, and a shot of hope sprang through my chest, I answered without even processing the name.

"Hello?"

"What's wrong?"

"Iris?" I asked in a whisper as my heart crumpled further. She felt it, too.

"Something's wrong. What's wrong?" The worry in her voice bled through the line.

"It's over," was all I could manage to process into words.

"What is?"

"Love." With that, the sob broke through and tears erupted as my heart gave one last crack before shattering into bitter shards.

CHAPTER 28

Lincoln
A month later

STARED DOWN AT MY PHONE, AT THE ELEVEN MISSED CALLS. Nine were from my new temporary assistant. The other two weren't Ivy. Her number hadn't come up on my phone since that day. No calls, no texts, and it had been the hardest thing in my life to not contact her.

With my final words, I made sure she wouldn't want anything to do with me. She didn't know, didn't understand, that everything I did, every word I spewed at her, was all for her protection.

I still couldn't decide if it was better or worse having Dante ten feet away staring at us. Probably for the better as I used my anger for him and unleashed it on her. It was the only way, and I made sure he saw every nasty, vile word I spewed at her. That he believed every lie just as she did.

A groan left me as I stared out on the sea of vultures circling our meeting place. Somehow they'd gotten wind I would be there, probably my shit for brains temporary assistant. At least the intern, Stacey, had molded into someone useful. She'd really stepped up in the wake of Ivy's departure. She watched my melt down that day, stared at me as I lost all composure, and she knew—it was all real.

Since then she'd worked to keep my downward spiral from prying eyes, and developed a bit of a backbone. It still had some growing to do, but every week I watched her get stronger and gain more confidence.

"Mr. Devereux! Lincoln! Can you tell us—"

"Lincoln, is it true Dante Kilgore stole from—"

"Mr. Devereux, how does it feel to be the savior in all this?"

I stopped at that last one and turned to the reporter. "I'm not a savior." Then, I continued my way into the restaurant.

For weeks I'd been hounded by the press, all wanting to know what happened, what went down, and why I became involved. Keeping my mouth shut was getting more and more difficult with each passing day.

Everything in my life was more difficult, even breathing, because Ivy wasn't by my side.

I slid into the seat across from Marcus and ignored the way his nose crinkled and his eyes widened.

"Have you been drinking? You look like hell."

"Every day since I last saw her," I admitted.

He shook his head. "I told you not to get attached to her. She was supposed to be collateral damage, and now you have me jumping through a dozen hoops to keep her name out of people's mouths."

"How much longer?" I asked, not caring what he said, as long as he was doing his job.

"Trials take time, and this case is still in its infancy, Lincoln.

This is going to go on for a while."

"How much longer until I can see her? I don't give a shit about all this." I waved my hand at the press waiting outside the restaurant.

He rubbed at his chin. "I'd give it at least six months. A year would be better."

My stomach dropped. "Six *more* months? Are you fucking kidding me? It's been a month, and I can barely function. You expect me to stay away from her for another six months? You're out of your goddamn mind."

"What does it matter?" he asked as he glared at me. It wasn't the first time he expressed his anger over my feelings for Ivy. "She hates you. What difference will six months make?"

I reached out, stealing the glass of whiskey that sat in front of him and threw it back before signaling to the waiter for two more.

"All the difference. She doesn't know. I did what you asked. I made sure there was no contact with her at all. I broke her, and she has no idea why. I'm not going to let her stew for six more months."

If I had to wait that long, not only would I lose her, but I would probably lose my position as CEO. The celebration of finally nailing Dante was crushed by the loss of Ivy, and I'd been in a tailspin ever since. Dan had to force me to leave a few times after that first week. He and Stacey were able to cover up what was going on, but every time I walked into my office, there were reminders of her everywhere. Ivy was still there in every corner.

I fed the depression with more alcohol than I'd consumed in the year prior combined. It was the first time I felt a depression like that all my own that wasn't connected to London and it was debilitating.

"You didn't want her implicated."

I slammed my hand down on the table. "Because she did nothing wrong."

Marcus remained unfazed by my outburst. His finger tapped on the tabletop. "This is the price. No contact. If you do, if his lawyers find out you're in contact with her, they will pull her into this, and they will drag her through the mud."

"They already know we were in a relationship. Dante told them that much." I scratched at my beard that had grown over the last month. I'd always been clean shaven, no more than a five o'clock shadow, but I'd given up caring. It wasn't the only thing that slipped.

"But Dante watched you get rid of her. They know she was the one who passed on information, and they have no legal standing since there was no NDA with Kilgore. But if Dante sees you with her, he will have them eat her alive out of spite."

"Is there really no other way?" I asked, hating the conversation with every fiber of my being.

"Lincoln, I have done *everything* to keep her off the table, but I know they are sniffing around, searching for anything. Right now, she isn't in their spotlight, but that could change at any moment."

I froze. "What do you mean that could change?"

Marcus looked around the room, then narrowed his eyes at me. "She was Dante's right hand for five years."

"She was his assistant," I clarified, not liking the direction of his words.

He blew out an exasperated breath. "I can't promise you anything, but be prepared."

The hackles rose on the back of my neck. "What the fuck

does that even mean? You promised, you said she'd be clear."

"And she is on our side, but his lawyers…"

"Fuck!" My heart slammed wildly in my chest. No. I did it all for a reason, for her. "Why didn't you tell me?"

"I'm telling you now."

"When it does me no good," I shouted.

"It kept you away from her, and this information in no way negates what I said earlier. Stay away. If there is no contact, they are less likely to show interest in her. But if you do, well, you know Dante better than most and know full well what he is capable of."

"Thanks a fucking lot, Marcus," I spat as I stood, tossing a few bills down before walking away.

I did know what Dante was capable of, and though I tried to deny it, I also knew the lengths he would go to displace the blame. Ivy wasn't safe from his deviousness, despite the show I gave him.

Everything I had done to protect her was going down the damn drain. My sacrifice could be for naught.

If Marcus kept me away from her for another six months, I would *never* get back the only woman I'd ever loved.

"What do I do, Koa?" I asked as I looked out on the Sound from my balcony. I was desperately in need of advice from my baby sister. She'd been my constant since everything went down, and the new information was just as hard for her to swallow. Still, that didn't make her response any less Koa-like.

"It's your bed, brother. Lie in it, and pray in a few months that she'll understand."

"I don't know if I can last a few months without her," I admitted. I always thought I was strong, that I was the light that could pull London from the dark. But the black swallowed me whole, and there was no light at the bottom. The dark was thick and heavy, and I wondered how long I could bear it before I gave in.

Was that what went through London's mind in her last days? Was what I was feeling the same?

"I'm not losing you, Linc. I won't."

I couldn't argue with her, because even hope had abandoned me. All my talk was just that when the agony sunk its teeth into my soul.

"I can't live without her."

"Then you need to get your knee pads out, explain to her what's going on, and let her make the decision on her own. She's a grown-ass woman, and pretty feisty from what you've told me."

And there it was. The spark, a small ray of light, of hope that swam through the darkness and enveloped me.

If I could get her to listen, if I told her why, maybe I could undo some of the pain. Maybe she would open back up to me, even just a little.

But it would require another sacrifice.

The deepest secret I owned.

The last secret.

CHAPTER 29

Ivy

"CAN YOU TELL ME WHY YOU WANT TO WORK FOR US?" the woman asked.

I couldn't even tell you what number interview I was at because just like all the others all I saw was a figure sitting on the other side of the table. I didn't even care about where I was or what position I applied for—there was only one I ever loved, and it was gone.

"Because you're as far removed from Lincoln Devereux as I can get," I replied, cursing myself for even bringing his name up.

The manager blinked at me. "I'm sorry, I don't understand."

"Of course not." I stood and held out my hand. "Thank you for meeting with me, but I don't think this is going to work out."

She blinked at me, her movements stunted from confusion.

I grabbed my purse and headed out. It was another in a line of self-sabotaged interviews. I couldn't work for any companies in competition with DCS for two years, per the non-compete clause in my contract. Which left me wondering where I did want to work.

I had time to figure it out. There was still a good amount of savings I'd built up in my account, and I qualified for unemployment, which was surprising considering the way Lincoln threw me out. I half expected him to deny it. Then again, the bastard had the gall to write the best letter of recommendation I'd ever read. It showed up in the mail the week after he fired me.

I ripped it up and threw it away.

I didn't need his help, or so I thought. With all the press, my resume had become tainted.

Every day I considered calling up Mike Deacon, but I was beginning to think Seattle was no longer where I belonged.

Iris was trying to convince me to move back to Indiana, and I was days if not hours from caving in and going for it. I needed a fresh start, somewhere away from Dante and Lincoln. Somewhere that I wasn't used over and over like a stupid, ignorant airhead. I stayed only to be hit again and again, thinking Lincoln would be different, but in the end, he wasn't.

꩜

A few days later as I left the office supply store, there was a magazine on the rack that made me stop. My heart jumped, then tightened at the soft, hazel eyes of my former boss and lover. I bought a copy, then proceeded to rip the cover up, earning some strange looks from the employee and other customers, but I didn't care. I simply asked for a trash can before throwing the pieces in and heading out the door.

The day after Lincoln fired me, the papers were littered with his face. Whatever exploded between him and Dante that day, whatever Lincoln had done, set off a string of investigations against Dante. Clients flooded from Dante to Lincoln, who was touted as the savior.

Only I knew it was all a lie. I knew the price paid, because it was me. An unknown currency in a revenge war that one side didn't even know was going on.

I still had no idea how it happened, only that Lincoln lied to me. He made me love him. Made me want a future with him, and he destroyed everything inside me.

But it didn't matter anymore. I was gone.

I had done it—I gave my apartment manager notice. With nothing keeping me in Seattle other than a love for the city, I decided to go back home. Iris had a second bedroom she was going to clear out for me, and most of my stuff would fit—thanks to my studio living—some things I would sell before I left. The rest could be stored at my dad's house for the time being.

It was time to start fresh, to start over. Mending the damage Lincoln had done was going to take time, and I was ready to be back with people who loved and supported me. I would miss my friends here, most of whom I'd sadly lost touch with while I was working hellish hours for DCS.

I pulled into my spot and finagled the flat boxes from the backseat. There was still so much to do to get my things moved two thousand miles, like figuring out how to get everything there. Briar was willing to drive his truck and we could rent a trailer, but that was a long, multi-day drive each way. I really thought he was willing because he really wanted to punch Lincoln in the face, and if he came, I wasn't sure I would try to stop him.

From a distance I could see someone leaning against the exterior wall of my apartment, next to the door leading to the interior hall. He wasn't wearing a suit, but jeans and a black T-shirt, a short beard framing his face. He pushed off the wall when he saw me coming.

A ripple moved through me when our eyes met, even from fifty feet away. My heart started thumping in my chest as a million questions moved through my mind.

"What do you want, Lincoln?" I asked from the foot of the steps leading to the second floor.

"To talk."

"I have nothing to talk about with you," I said as I ascended the stairs.

"Yes, you do."

Every step made my chest hurt more. Walking toward him was torture. I should have gone through the other door, but he would have just followed. "And what's that?"

"How bad my coffee has been since you've been gone."

The closer I got, the worse looking he got. What had he done with himself?

Don't, Ivy. Don't. He's a lying asshole, remember?

"Sounds like karma to me."

"Ivy," He glanced down at the cardboard under my arm. "What's going on?"

"I have to be out in two weeks."

"Out? What do you mean? Where are you going?"

I blew out a breath in agitation. "What does it matter to you? Go away, Mr. Devereux."

"It matters a fucking lot."

"I'm going home. Happy? Now leave."

He shook his head. "No. No fucking way. You can't go."

"You can't tell me what to do anymore, remember?"

"You really fucking can't."

"Oh, yes, I can. Move." I pushed at his chest but he stayed still, blocking the door.

"Not before I talk with you. Please, Ivy. I need to talk with you."

"No, you don't. Get out of here. I don't ever want to see you again, Lincoln. Fuck off!" I shoved him aside, gaining access to the door.

His hand slammed down against the door frame, blocking me in. "Do you have any idea how hard it has been for me to stay away?"

His words lit a fire in me. "Stay away? Oh, I imagine it's been easy for you, or have you forgotten what you said to me?"

He glanced around before leaning in, his voice low. "Let's talk inside."

"Do you really think I'm going to let you in?" I spat at him.

"Please," he begged. "I need to explain."

"No need there. I already know you're an asshole. Besides, what more do I need to know? You used me, and then you threw me away. No wonder that position sat empty for as long as it did. You had this planned the whole time, didn't..." I blew out a hard breath. "You know what? Never mind. It doesn't fucking matter. Go away."

Suddenly, his lips were on mine, the boxes dropping to the floor. It set off that spark. The one I only ever had with him. His kiss brought it all back. The longing for him that I thought I'd buried came flooding in, and my heart ripped even more.

I pushed back on him, my hand lashing across his face.

We were both breathing hard when he turned back to me, his eyes dark.

"I deserved that."

"Damn right," I said through gritted teeth. It took all of my strength to keep the tears that were flooding my eyes from falling.

"I'm so sorry I hurt you, but it had to be done."

I leaned over and picked up the boxes. "It doesn't matter."

"Yes, it does."

I turned back to him. "Why?"

His jaw ticked and he looked around again, his eyes darting. "Inside, please."

In all the months I'd worked with him, I could probably count the amount of times he said please to me on one hand, and in the few short minutes of him in front of me, he had surpassed that. The only reason I even considered letting him in was because of that one word, and his nervousness that confused me.

We entered and I set the boxes down, then turned to him.

"Okay, you're inside. Start talking," I said as I folded my arms in front of me. "You have five minutes, Mr. Devereux."

"I came to beg your forgiveness for what I said, for what I did, and I need you to know my feelings for you were never fake," he said in one breath. "It had to be a swift cut."

I stared at him as I attempted to process what he just said and whether or not I believed a single word. "Why?"

"Because I needed you to think I didn't care about you, that I had no feelings for you, to keep you away."

"Banner job there," I said with a harsh laugh.

"But it's the furthest from the truth." His voice was low, calling me to look him in the eye. There was something there, something that scared me more than anything.

"Are you going to say something like—"

"I love you, Ivy."

The floor fell out from beneath me, my knees suddenly weak. They were words I'd dreamed of hearing, but words I refused to believe. "You're lying."

Our eyes were locked as I desperately searched for the lie, the falsity of his words.

He simply shook his head. "When Dante showed up, I knew what was about to happen. I'd been planning it for months. Years, actually. What I hadn't planned was you."

The last sentence repeated in my mind. "You used me, Lincoln."

He nodded. "Yes."

"Tell me why."

"Revenge," he said simply before elaborating. "I really was looking for an assistant, and you truly were the best applicant. I admit, I had thought of hiring you simply for what information I could get from you, but when I saw you, I wanted you close to me and far from him."

"You're an asshole," I spat. My emotions were all over the place, but I needed to remind him of my anger.

"Yes."

"You lied to me." I pushed against his chest, making him step back. "You used me." I hit him again as tears filled my eyes and began to slide down my cheeks as everything crumbled. "I loved you, and it was all a lie!"

His arms wrapped around me, and he held me tight to him. Pain tore at my chest from his touch. It was too much, but he held me fast and I couldn't escape.

"It wasn't a lie. My feelings for you...I didn't want to face their strength, to face how much I love you. I knew they were there, but I had no idea how deep they ran until he was standing in front of me."

"Because you knew what you were doing."

He pulled back and gently moved a few strands of hair from my face, his thumb swiping at the tears. "I did."

For a month, all I wanted to know was why, and as he stood in front of me, I could feel the hesitation that lingered below the surface. "What was so important that you had to destroy me?"

"Destroying Dante."

My brow scrunched. Kilgore couldn't compare to DCS. Even the software they created that Dante ran off with didn't seem to warrant such a long and elaborate plan. There was something else. "Why?"

There was a pause and that look I knew all too well flitted across his face. It was another secret, perhaps the deepest one.

"Because he killed London."

I drew in a sharp breath, my eyes wide. *What?* My heart seemed to shatter again, but it wasn't for me, but for him. I knew some of their history, knew that once upon a time they were close, but Dante a killer of his twin sister?

"He may not have physically put the knife to her wrists, but mentally he fucked her up. Little by little he broke her."

My head shook back and forth. "I don't understand."

His brow furrowed, eyes filled with so much torment. "I've never told anyone this."

"Well, you're going to need to, because your five minutes are up." It hurt to say, but I needed to be as sharp with him as he was with me. If he wanted a second chance, I needed to know everything.

"I met Dante in college, as you knew, but so did London. We were friends, did a lot together. After college, London and I moved back to Colorado. I got a job with Central Designs, and a few years later, so did Dante. It was great having him there, and we were working hard on creating something huge when he and London got close." He pulled in a settling breath.

My stomach dropped as something in the back of my mind began to click.

"I didn't mind because Dante was a good guy, and London was happy. A few years later, Dante decided to move back to Seattle, and he took London with him. He also stole my drive with the software we created. He said he wanted to tweak it, and for London's sake, I let it go."

Oh, God no. My stomach sank further, because I knew. I finally knew.

"He stole her, knowing full well what it would do to us both, but he had her wrapped around his finger and used her desire to get married against her. After they moved, I started to hear things. When I talked to her, she assured me she was happy." He clenched his fist and tapped in on his chest, over his heart. "But I could *feel* it. Cold, dark vines that infested me like a virus. I didn't understand at the time, I just thought it was the stress of my new position, of working on all the promises I made to Cameo International, or from being away from my twin for the first time in my life."

Tears filled his eyes, his bottom lip trembling as he drew in a steadying breath. It was obvious by the raw emotion coming from him it was a topic he never spoke of, let alone thought about. Just remembering that she was gone was hard enough on him.

"Every time I talked to her, I probed her, but she said everything was fine, even when I could tell it wasn't. We got into a few fights about it." His jaw tightened, his eyes hardened, and the agony turned into a blazing pit of fire. "It wasn't until after she was gone that I found out how he'd become verbally abusive to her, was cheating on her, lying to her, just breaking her down until she couldn't take it anymore. He cut her off from everything and everyone, including me, and showed he had no real desire to marry her or anyone else. Her depression skyrocketed, so bad there was no trying to process her pain."

Everything clicked into place. All that I had learned about him, all of his secrets, weren't separate things, but all connected. The hatred for Dante, the call when he snatched the phone from my hand and his reaction. Everything stemmed from Dante.

He paused as he gathered himself. "Dante didn't even care when it happened, no sadness, no remorse. A few weeks later I also found out he sold the software without my knowledge or consent. When I confronted him, he touted that London knew, that her remorse for not telling me was the reason she did it. Maybe she did feel guilt, but that wasn't why, because she knew there was nothing that could ever stop me from loving her."

Dante stole their joint software and sold it for millions. Dante ruined his twin sister and drove her to suicide. Dante was the villain in Lincoln's life.

"The connection—that's why you felt so down." I wanted to ease his pain. The agony radiating from him wouldn't be denied. It was infectious, and I actually hurt for him. Even when he told me about London, I'd never seen Lincoln so vulnerable. He was shaking, but it didn't stop him from cupping my cheek.

"When she died, so did I. But you revived me, Ivy. You brought me back to life."

A lone tear fell, sliding down my cheek. It was so hard to not comfort him because the hurt he inflicted still resonated inside me. I wasn't ready to give in with just a few words, even with as devastating of a confession as it was.

"So is everything better now that Dante is in jail. Is that what you're doing here?" There was more than a bit of spite in my tone. I felt for him, for what Dante did to him, but what he did to me—was it any better?

"No, it's not better, and it's not going to be for a long time."

"Then why are you here?" I asked as I stared down at my hand that rested over his chest. How had I allowed him to keep holding me?

"I'm here because I can't spend another day without you. I'm here against the advice of counsel because I love you, Ivy. I can't stand to be apart any longer." He cupped my face, tilting my head back to look at him before falling to his knees. "You are a queen, and I am but a humble king at your feet, begging for your forgiveness, and for you to smile down at me."

My bottom lip trembled as I looked down at him, tears filling my eyes. "You're a stupid king, Lincoln Devereux."

He nodded. "The worst."

"And you really deserve a swift kick in the balls."

He let out a pained groan. "If that's what it takes to have you in my arms again, do it."

I was tempted, but there was still the fact that he pushed me away. "But what about all of your reasoning? Protecting me?"

His expression morphed, a wave of fear passing over as he stood again. "If you forgive me, if you want to be with me, there are potential consequences."

"What kind?"

"Dante's team of lawyers has more than once tried to put some of the blame on you."

I froze. "What?"

"We've managed to shoot them down so that nothing has made it through, but if they find out about us, I can't stop it anymore. You will be pulled in, questioned, deposed, hounded by press—it's not a fun experience. They'll dissect you and your family, our relationship, attack you on the most personal levels. They will pursue any avenue to put some of what he did onto you in order to lessen the blow."

Lessen the blow? My mind whirled. Would Dante really do that? Would he try to put some of what he did back on me? Would he say I was helping him?

The answer was yes, the son-of-a-bitch would.

"I don't understand. Why me? I mean, I get the part about being the unknowing informant, though I wasn't as unknowing as you think."

"What do you mean?"

"I made the conscious decision to tell you. There was nothing stopping me but my own moral code and a small string of respect for my former position, but once you told me about London, that was gone."

"Then the why would be simple—because you are with me. You were unconquerable in his world, but not with me."

He was right. If I was beside Lincoln, the answer was a definite yes that Dante would attack me. He hated Lincoln. I knew that before I went to work for him.

I stepped out of his arms and pulled my phone from my purse, earning a confused look from him.

"What are you doing?"

"Fact checking," I replied as I typed in London Devereux into the search bar.

"You don't believe or trust me?"

I hit the search icon. "I'm not sure of anything right now,

so give me this."

It took no time at all to bring up her photo, ones I'd seen, ones with Lincoln.

Ones with Dante.

I clicked a link to her Facebook profile. It was in memory, but I could still scroll down to what I was looking for, posts from almost a decade before. I stopped at the familiar but younger version of Dante. A photo of him with London, a diamond ring on her finger, smiles on their faces with a caption of "Look who just got engaged." It was dated just over a year before she died. After that, posts of them moving to Seattle, and then things began to change. What had been a happy profile started turning dark. Posts asking where she was, posts of people missing her, then the "Heaven gained an angel" posts started. Not one from Dante since they'd moved, not even a tag from London or anyone else.

But there were from Lincoln.

It wasn't his name, but the poster Andrew Lincoln was him—Lincoln Andrew Devereux. There was no photos and his profile was private, but her page was littered with posts from him over the vacant years.

"Andrew Lincoln."

"That's me," he confirmed. "It's a striped profile—no friends, no photos. I keep it to visit London. I can't...I can't let go of our conversations, our posts. I talk to her, look for answers."

"What are the questions?"

He blew out a breath. "Were the signs there and I just didn't notice? Was there something hidden in her words? Was there anything I could have done?"

The only thing he could have done was to have never met

Dante Kilgore, but it seemed there was no avoiding it. I scanned through her wall, looking at all the posts by Lincoln and was surprised at the most recent one: *I met someone. She's special, and you would love her, like I do. I wish you were here to meet her. I miss you, Lolo.*

It was dated and location tagged during our trip to Rome. Again, tears streamed down my face. He told his sister about me in the only way he could, told her his feelings.

"He manipulated her," I said as I wiped at the wetness coating my face. Lincoln nodded in agreement as he grabbed me some tissue for my nose. "He is a manipulator, Lincoln. That's what he does to everyone. He does it to you even now."

"How so?"

"Because he got you to hurt me. And that hurt you."

"It devastated me," he choked out. "I can't sleep, I can't eat. I barely work. I just drink and try to dull the pain while I pray that you will forgive me. I wanted to keep you safe, because I know what he's capable of. If anything ever happened to you...I'm at my ultimate weakest right now, Ivy. My lowest point. Everything I've worked for means nothing without you in my life."

I choked back a sob. "Stupid king," I said as I stepped forward and placed my hand on his chest. "I've always been your queen."

His eyes widened as they searched mine, flickering between them before he leaned in close and slowly, gently, pressed his lips to mine. It was the hit to my chest I needed, the restart of my broken heart.

"I guess we should talk about how this is going to go over dinner," I said. "Because if that bastard thinks he's going to come after me for being with you, I've got a lot more of his dirty little secrets up my sleeve."

"Does that mean..." he trailed off, a hopeful glint in his eye.

"It means dinner, and we'll see about dessert."

A smile spread on his face as relief washed over him. He crashed into me, his lips devouring mine, and I let myself feel it all. Nothing was perfect or the way it was, but maybe something from the war was salvageable.

CHAPTER 30

Lincoln

INCOLN DEVEREUX TAKES A VACATION SHOULD HAVE BEEN the headline of the newspaper.

In eight years, I had accumulated forty weeks of unused vacation time. Meaning I had used a whopping two personal/vacation days a year on average, the rest rolling over.

Imagine the surprise when I cleared my calendar for the first time in nearly a decade and took an entire week off. Even more surprising was that I was thinking of taking the following week off as well.

Not only that, it was a staycation—at home—and my phone, tablet, and computer stayed off. I had a new plan, a new goal.

Dinner with Ivy turned into dessert that turned into seven beautiful days and six bliss-filled nights.

"Do you forgive me yet?" I asked as I fingered her. She was on the verge of another orgasm, and I wasn't above using them to get her to concede.

"So close," she said in a breathy moan, her back arching against my chest.

I didn't know which she was talking about, but both were important.

I watched for her cues, the intonations, and found the spot that made her writhe. Her scream echoed around the tile walls of the bathroom as she came, her back arching against my chest. She relaxed back into me, a satiated smile on her face.

"Isn't this a nice big tub?" I asked.

"Mm hmm." Her eyes were closed, completely blissed out, making it the perfect time to start the conversation I'd been itching to have all week.

"Huge two-person shower."

"What are you getting at, Mr. Devereux?" she asked groggily.

"Just commenting. Nice big bathroom, huge closet with lots of room."

"Enough cryptic-ness." She slapped at my hand, which barely connected under the water.

"I'm just pointing it out," I said with a coy smile.

She simply hummed as she turned and wrapped her arms around my shoulders before leaning in. Her lips were so soft against mine, tongue light and fruity from the strawberries we'd eaten.

My hands traveled down her sides, around her waist until I was cupping her gorgeous ass, squeezing it as my hips flexed against her. With one sharp tug I pulled her up, grabbed my cock, and pushed her back down.

A deep groan left me at the feel of her warmth enveloping me. If I wasn't in complete bliss, I would have been smiling at the way her eyes popped wide, her mouth dropping open as she drew in a shuddered breath.

"Linc...oln," she managed to choke out.

"Mmm, yes?"

Her fingers flexed against my skin as her hips rotated, pushing me deeper. A moan crawled out of her chest as her hips slowly rose until I was almost all the way out, then equally, teasingly slow, slid back down.

"Why do you feel so perfect inside me?"

Her hips rose, and she began an achingly slow and steady rhythm.

"Because you were made just for me."

"I was," she said so low I almost didn't hear.

As she moved up and down, the water began to slosh around the tub, splashing and crashing over the edge onto the floor. The faster she worked her hips, the closer I got, and the more water worked its way out.

Instead of the clapping of our skin together, it was soapy whitecaps of bath water sounding against the walls. Each stroke up and down was a bigger tease than the last, making me harder with every one. Chest to chest, heart to heart, every care was gone, our focus on each other.

With my hands, I guided her. With her hands she gripped, holding on as my hips joined in, pushing deeper. It was messy, wet perfection. Water splashed between us, but we didn't care. Ivy leaned in and the waves around us lessened, her lips a breath away from my own.

"I forgive you," she whispered against my lips.

It was like a lightning bolt shot through me, and without warning, I exploded inside her in an almost violent reaction. Everything went white, my muscles coiled tight as I came, each spurt landing deep inside her. My vice-like grip kept her in place until she milked the last drop, and I relaxed back against the tub.

"Fuck, Ivy," I said between heavy breaths.

She nipped at my neck. "I really do like this tub."

"Me too."

We stayed in the water, my arms wrapped around her, until the water turned cold. A quick rinse off in the shower and, regrettably, Ivy put on some clothes. While it was only a cute little sleep set, I still lamented the loss of her nakedness.

My gaze lingered, watching as she moved around my room with such ease and comfort, something that worked to my advantage.

It was almost fitting that Ivy was the same age I was when I lost London. My world stopped then. Any forward movement of my life was frozen as I focused on one task.

With that done, with allowing myself to move forward, it felt like I was starting over from back then. As if my life was on pause, and I was picking it back up. In a way, that was true.

The nearly nine years that separated us in age never seemed to be any sort of issue, and I wondered if that was why—I had not evolved much over that time.

With Ivy life began again, and I wanted to experience it all with her. I wanted her to live with me, to one day become my wife and someday the mother of my children.

I had thoughts of a future, of a family, no longer frozen in the past.

"I want to show you something," I said as I held out my hand.

"What's that?"

"A room."

"I've seen them all," she said with a scrunched brow.

After a week with me she had seen most areas, but not

all. I'd managed to keep her distracted from thinking about her apartment that she had given notice on. One week was all we would need to gather it all up and move it in. That was, if she said yes.

"There are still areas you haven't seen," I said as I directed her to the second bedroom. I opened the door across from the master suite and flipped on the lights.

"What's this?" she asked as she peered into the empty room. There was nothing in it, and no need to have anything. Visitors never happened and whenever my parents made a trip up, they stayed with Koa.

"This could be your space or a nursery."

"A nursery?"

I wrapped my arms around her waist and held her close. "Not now, but one day. I want all that life has to offer with you, including a life we make together."

She turned in my arms, her eyes filled with tears. "Lincoln."

"If and when the press finds out about your involvement, you'll be safe here. No one will be able to get in. They can't touch you here."

She let out a sigh. I knew there were things she wanted to talk to Marcus about, information she wanted to directly convey, and, in time, that would open the flood gates. I would use any means necessary to protect her, but I knew it wasn't possible to hide her from everything coming.

Ivy was the strongest woman I knew, and whatever was coming her way, she could handle it, especially if we were together.

"I love you."

"Is that a yes?" I asked, my heart stopping to hear her confirmation.

She nodded. "Yes."

I blew out a breath. "Good, because my other alternative was one of two things—kidnapping, or keeping you in a constant orgasmic state."

"Well, that last one doesn't sound so bad."

"I plan to do that one anyway." I grinned at her.

We walked into the kitchen, and I pulled out a bottle of water and handed it to her. "What sounds good for lunch?"

"Is it lunch time?" she asked as she looked to the clock.

Not only had we lost track of days, but time slipped away as well. Getting lost in Ivy was the best way to lose myself.

"So, what's going to happen now?"

"What do you mean?" I asked as I pulled up options for lunch on my phone.

"Do I get to come back and work for you?"

I blew out a breath and leaned forward, resting my forehead against hers. "Not yet."

"Why not?" she asked, her brow scrunched.

"I was told to stay away from you for more than six months. Therefore, six months."

She balked at me. "What am I supposed to do for all that time?"

"I'm not sure."

Her mouth turned down. "You weren't thinking past this week, were you?"

"You tend to make me want to live in the moment."

She rolled her eyes, but she couldn't stop the smile. "What am I going to do for all those moments?"

"There are some assistant duties you can do from here," I offered.

"Some things can definitely be done from here."

"There's also another thing you could do."

"And that is?" she pressed.

"Plan a wedding."

A gasp left her, her eyes wide. "What?"

Not exactly the way I meant to propose, or even the right time, but neither of those made it wrong.

"I hadn't meant to ask right now. I'm a bit unprepared. It doesn't make it any less true. I can't be without you, Ivy. I don't want to be without you ever again."

"But we've barely been a couple," she argued.

It was cute she thought rationale would win out in the situation, but it wouldn't. Every ounce of blood, every cell, knew with certainty she was meant to be with me, to be my wife, for always.

"We've almost been apart as long as we were together."

"Nothing has ever made as much sense in my life as you. I never told you, but you are my perfect storm—everything I ever wanted in a woman all wrapped up in one. From the moment we met, something clicked into place inside me."

"With me, too."

"Then who is to say it's too early?"

"Me."

"Are you saying you're going to make me wait again?" I asked.

"Yes," she said as she pulled my head down closer to her lips, "but at least this time I'll warm your bed."

EPILOGUE

Lincoln
One year later

"THE LONG LEGAL BATTLE OF DANTE KILGORE CAME to a close yesterday. The former CEO of Kilgore Industries was found guilty on multiple accounts. Sentencing to be announced on Thursday. The now dismantled company was found to be in violation of multiple privacy policies, including HIPPA violations, through the software created and maintained by his company. Kilgore was also found guilty of tax evasion, fraud, and embezzlement. Rival businessman Lincoln Devereux, CEO of Data Consolidation Solutions, was a key factor in the case against him. Devereux passed information he received from multiple sources to the authorities, who began the investigation that was the demise of Kilgore Industries. When asked why he was compelled to contact the authorities, Devereux answered with a cryptic 'Karma at its finest.'"

"I wonder what happened between them."

"Who knows, but I don't think I want to get on his bad side," the commentator said with a laugh.

"True. Coming up next—"

I shut the TV off and leaned back in my chair. So much had happened in the past year, so much had changed. The biggest was the door closing on my near decade-long quest for revenge. I achieved my goal of making Dante pay and set a new goal to be happy, to have love. A goal I was determined to strive for every single day.

The biggest part of that was Ivy. We'd managed to keep her away from the media as much as possible, but in the end, she was forced to testify. We didn't watch the news for weeks after as they dug into her.

At the grocery store, she caught a glimpse of her face in the newspaper. She bought it, took it outside, and lit it on fire in protest.

Life with her was always interesting. Her reactions and insight surprised me every day, even after a year of her living with me. By the time the third month rolled around, she got stir crazy and coerced me to go back to being my in-office, full-time assistant with the best damn blow job I'd ever had in my life, Working me to the edge and refusing to let me come until I agreed.

Apparently working from home wasn't enough. Even letting her take over decorating, making the space as much hers as mine, didn't fill her days enough.

There were still forty-two pictures of London on the walls, per my request, but she spread them out between the rooms and incorporated photos of us. A little paint change, some softer fabrics and colors, and in the end, it felt a lot more like a home instead of a fortress.

She didn't make the spare bedroom into her space, instead taking over the smaller living room off the kitchen, claiming to like the view better. The bedroom was converted into a guest space for when Iris or her dad came for a visit.

I took a sip from the cup on my desk and immediately searched for a place to spit it out that wasn't all over the documents covering my desk. The trash can was luckily empty, and I expelled the foul, cold brew into the garbage.

Blindly, I reached for the phone and dialed Ivy's extension. "Get me some coffee."

"Sir?" she asked in a tone I knew so well. She liked to remind me that manners mattered. Barking orders at her would not be tolerated.

I groaned and cleared my throat. "I'm sorry. My coffee has gone cold. Would you please get me a fresh cup?"

"Right away, Mr. Devereux."

My dick twitched at the sultry way she said my name. Knowing her well, she did it on purpose.

I'd glanced back to the contract I was going over when the door clicked open and she entered. I was entranced at the way her hips swayed, hypnotized by the way her bump rocked back and forth.

"You used to watch my breasts like that. What happened?" she asked as she stepped around my desk and stopped in front of me.

"I knocked you up." I reached up and smoothed my hands across her stomach before placing a kiss over the center. "My dick gets hard every time I see it sticking out between your hips, knowing I did that." She was at twenty weeks and her stomach had just really started to pop out in the past few weeks.

The baby was a happy but unexpected addition to our relationship and completely my fault. Yes, it was something we planned to do one day, but life decided it would be a little earlier. Ivy had missed her appointment due to the trial, and every time she'd reschedule for months had the same result. She ran out of birth control, and I continued coming in her as much as I could.

I pulled her to my lap and she leaned down, pressing her lips to mine.

"Lunch?"

I slipped my hand between her thighs and rubbed the knuckle of my thumb across her clit, making her draw in a breath. "Dessert first?"

"Incorrigible." She laughed. "I would take you up on that, but the alien in my stomach wants actual food before you go knocking on his door."

"Her door, you mean."

She rolled her eyes. "Hers, his, whatever."

"Next week, right?" I asked, though I knew. I'd been counting down the days until I found out if we had a little prince or princess coming.

She nodded. "Tuesday."

I fiddled with the large diamond ring on her finger. The ring I'd placed there six months ago, before the baby. "Are you sure I can't convince you to get married before the baby comes?"

"There's no time to plan a wedding with our schedule and getting ready for the baby."

Ivy was adamant that she wanted to continue being my assistant after we married and even after the baby was born. It was one of the few things we argued over, because I wanted her to be a stay-at-home mom. Money wasn't an issue. She didn't need to work, but she wanted to. She reminded me that just because she was going to be a mother didn't mean she wasn't also Ivy.

She also reminded me that my equally workaholic little sister was going to continue working and expanding her company after Jase Lincoln Ackerman joined the world. Koa was a few months further along in her pregnancy, and I was excited about our child having a cousin close in age. My parents had even decided to move up to Seattle in order to be closer to their grandchildren and were due to arrive in a few weeks.

Every day Ivy continued to amaze me.

"We can have a wedding at anytime."

"What are you saying?" she asked while giving me the side eye.

I placed a kiss on her neck. "I'm saying I will give you the biggest, most beautiful wedding you can ever dream of whenever you want, but can we please be legally married before then? Become Mrs. Devereux on paper. We can have a little celebratory dinner with Koa and Jack and my parents, and we can have the big ceremony a year later. I'll hire the best wedding coordinator."

"Well, Christmas is next month and I have been trying to figure out what to get you."

"A family would make a wonderful gift," I assured her with a smile.

"I'll miss you calling me Miss Prescot."

"But Mrs. Devereux sounds so much better," I said as I kissed up the length of her neck.

She let out a hum that vibrated against my lips.

In the end, Ivy wasn't the collateral damage. It was me.

She put me back together, helped me remember what life was all about. She was the savior of our story. The mighty queen protecting the fallen king and, in the end, ruling the kingdom together.

THE END

AFTER ALL THE WORDS AND THE STUFFS

Hello! You've finished! Congratulations! I really hope you enjoyed Lincoln and Ivy's story.

This was a new and different experience for me. For those who have read and followed all my works this is written a bit differently. This is also the first time I have written a book so quickly after the idea, and I'm going to totally blame Whitney G for that.

"Why? What did Whitney do?" you ask.

She wrote some fucking awesome office romance books, that's what she did!! And office romances are my favorite! I've owned Reasonable Doubt for YEARS and just never gotten to reading it, and after a convention this year I vowed to read more. So, from September to late October I read around four books (RD series counting as 1) and they were all office romances which made me want to write another as well.

This story didn't turn out ANYTHING like the original idea. The only thing that was the same was the boss/assistant aspect lol! In the original idea Lincoln was a total and complete asshole. Full of himself, narcissistic, and a man-whore—pretty much he was Dante, only better. Maybe one day that original idea will become another book, maybe not. My list of books to write is pretty long already!

Thank you so much for reading!

ACKNOWLEDGEMENTS

There are not enough thanks that I can give to Danielle, who was a huge help so many times during this process. From bouncing ideas off, to talking things out, to honesty and cheerleading, I could not have written it without you!

Always to my boo, Elena M Reyes—my constant support and BFF. Thank you for all your love.
To my hubby, for his continued support in all ways. I love you.

For Kandace... gone but never forgotten.

ABOUT THE AUTHOR

K.I. Lynn is the *USA Today* Bestselling Author from The Bend Anthology and the Amazon Bestsellers, *Breach* and *Becoming Mrs Lockwood*. She spent her life in the arts, everything from music to painting and ceramics, then to writing. Characters have always run around in her head, acting out their stories, but it wasn't until later in life she would put them to pen. It would turn out to be the one thing she was really passionate about.

Since she began posting stories online, she's garnered acclaim for her diverse stories and hard hitting writing style. Two stories and characters are never the same, her brain moving through different ideas faster than she can write them down as it also plots its quest for world domination...or cheese. Whichever is easier to obtain... Usually it's cheese.

Website—www.kilynnauthor.com
Facebook—www.facebook.com/kilynn.breach
Twitter—twitter.com/KI_Lynn_
Instagram—www.instagram.com/k.i.lynn
Get my Newsletter—http://bit.ly/1U9NSoC

MORE BOOKS FROM
K.I. LYNN

Welcome to the Cameo Hotel

I get what I want.

When I walked through the door of the Cameo Hotel I didn't expect such a beauty to be working the front desk.

The effect she has on me is intense, and I make her life a living hell because of it.

I love her spirit, her internal defiance when completing the most inane task I assign her. My two week stay has turned into unending, just to be near her.

She's under my every command if she wants to keep me happy.

There's one last thing I want.

Her.

Find out more here
books2read.com/WelcomeToTheCameoHotel

Cocksure

A life altering lie, ten years, and one wild night later, the game has changed.

Niko

My life is great. I love my job, have awesome friends, and a great family.

Women love me, even if they know it's just for a night.

I always thought love at first sight was bullshit. Then she came storming into my life. She tore through my every rule, rocked my world, and knocked me on my ass.

There's only one problem…she lied.+

Turns out my best friend's little sister isn't so little anymore.

Everly

I stole a night with my fantasy. Lied to him.

After ten years of not seeing each other, Niko doesn't even recognize me.

So I take what I want from him, what I need from him. Without worry. Without consequence.

What I didn't count on was the lingering need for him.

Once the truth is out, the game changes. There are consequences.

I should have known nothing in my life is ever simple.

My brother is going to kill his best friend and I have nine months to figure out what I want.

Find out more here: books2read.com/Cocksure-Lynn-Kelley

Becoming Mrs. Lockwood

Every girl has dreams of meeting Prince Charming, or at least I know I did.

A fairy tale-like meeting of love at first site.
Real life and fairy tales are very different.

I'm just a small town Indiana girl that had a chance encounter with one of Hollywood's golden boys. You may think you know where this story goes—not even close.

Life is different. Marriage is hard. It's even worse when you're strangers.

Find out more here: books2read.com/BecomingMrsLockwood

Six

I had a one-night stand. It wasn't my first, but it would be my last.

A gun to the head.

A trained killer.

A deadly conspiracy.

Kidnapped and on the run, my life and death is in the hands of a sadist captor who happens to be my one-night stand. Armed with countless weapons, money, and new identities, the man I call Six drags me around the world.

The manhunt is on and Six is the next target. Can we find out who is killing off the Cleaners before they find us?

Two down, seven to go.

When it's all over he'll finish the job that dropped him into my life, and end it.

Stockholm Syndrome meets bucket list, and the question of what would you do to live before you died. The questions aren't always answered in black and white. Gray becomes the norm as my morals are tested.

Death is a tragedy, and I'll do anything to stay alive.

Are you ready for the last ride of your life? Six has a gun to your head—what would you do?

This isn't a love story.

It's a death story.

Find out more here: books2read.com/Six-KILynn
Check out the Trailer—youtu.be/fzpON3PadIA

Breach, Book 1

Existence is more than just a word, it's a state of being. More importantly, it's my state of being. Day by day I go through the motions of living—eat, breathe, work, sleep.

That is until I finally get some help at work in the form of Nathan Thorne. He's sexy, cocky, arrogant, an asshole, and total bullshit.

I see through the façade to the turbulent man beneath, but I'm not the only one who can see through masks.

One late night the tension between us explodes, starting a lust filled craving for each other. All it takes is that night and his dirty talking mouth, and I'm his.

Now sex is in the mix. Violent and dirty and passionate and everything I need to fill the void inside me but one thing is missing—he can never love me.

It's not enough for me to leave, even though I know I should.

More than my heart is on the line, and I don't know if I'll survive our breach.

Find out more here: books2read.com/Breach

Need, Book 1

I was Kira's from the first moment I saw her. Maybe it was love at first sight, but I was only ten.

She became my best friend.

My crush.

The girl I can't live without.

But I have to.

She was almost mine, but my father took away my chance.

Now she lives across the hall from me. Instead of the title of girlfriend, she's now my stepsister.

But that doesn't stop how I feel, how I want her. Thankfully, I'm off to college two hundred miles away, but even that doesn't help.

She's under my skin, all around me, and I watch her morph from a sexy teenager to an irresistible woman.

I can't take it anymore, I need her.

Is it possible to ever be happy without the one person you *need*?

"I'm Brayden, baby. The man you've been dreaming about your whole life. And I'm about to fucking show you why."

Part 1 of a 3 part series.

Find out more here: books2read.com/NeedSeries

CPSIA information can be obtained
at www.ICGtesting.com
Printed in the USA
FSHW011527050420
68833FS